HER WORST MISTAKE

A ROSEMARY RUN THRILLER

KELLY UTT

PROLOGUE

A Year Prior, Back Then
Las Vegas, Nevada

It had been a long week. Amelia Baker had traveled to Sin City with her closest friend, Rebecca Tatum, to take her mind off of a bad breakup with the latest in a string of lackluster boyfriends. Amelia had grieved the end of her romantic relationship over mixed drinks and mixed company, most notably during late-night trysts after demure Rebecca had turned in each evening. By week's end, Amelia had bedded a handsome city slicker from New York City, a gritty motorcycle dude from rural Missouri, and-- most surprisingly, to her as much as anyone-- a sultry Vegas performer who wore little more than feathers to work each night and happened to be a woman.

Still in her thirties, Amelia was young enough to have a fit, attractive body that she could use to entice lovers, if she so chose. While in Vegas, she had dolled herself up for maximum effect, sparing no expense on her outfits, accessories, and makeup. She knew how to make herself look good by playing to her natural assets. Every detail of her appearance had been carefully cultivated-- tight-fitting tops to accentuate her slim figure and curvy chest, high-waisted jeans to make her ample backside swell at all the right angles, and low heels to highlight her shapely legs without adding too much height to her already tall 5'11" frame.

Amelia looked like a supermodel when she leaned into the swagger and strutted her stuff down Las Vegas Boulevard. It had worked like a charm. She had turned heads everywhere she went, and that was saying something given the plethora of beautiful women in the popular desert oasis. Amelia's deep chestnut-colored hair danced around her strong, yet delicate shoulders like a dark silky mane when she moved. She wore her locks long, the bottom strands brushing her perky breasts and teasing the men-- and women-- wishing for a glimpse of what lies underneath.

Fun didn't begin to describe the glitzy, sensuous nights Amelia had enjoyed. Dressing up in barely-there clothes and going out to party under the bright lights of the famous Las Vegas Strip had made her feel desirable, which in turn, gave her a sense of control over her life. She knew it wasn't real, but in the moment, that didn't matter. Locking eyes with a sexy stranger then negotiating the unspoken agreement to take each other's pain away was as addictive as any drug.

Sweet and innocent Rebecca had warned Amelia about partying too hard and getting herself in trouble.

Rebecca was a sensible soul, married to a cop back home in Rosemary Run and content to devote herself to being a wife and corporate career woman. She wouldn't be caught dead conducting herself like Amelia. It wasn't that she looked down on her friend, but rather that she simply had different sensibilities. Rebecca's idea of a good time involved things like game nights, bowling, and maybe a late-night movie or a day trip out of town if she was feeling adventurous. She wasn't a party girl. She didn't want to be.

Amelia kicked herself for having brought Rebecca to Las Vegas. She loved and admired her friend, but the pair were on totally different wavelengths about this sort of thing. Amelia had thought it would be fun to sit by the pool with Rebecca and try out a few of the great restaurants in the area, but she should have known herself well enough to realize she'd want more. She'd *need* more. Amelia had serious issues to work out. Not to mention, she had serious demons to entertain. Rebecca existed in a different world. One that didn't shy from the light of day or the honest truth. The two could never, ever overlap. Not really.

As the trip drew to a close, Amelia had begun to feel regretful and disenchanted with life. It had been frustrating to know that for all of the fun she'd had, nothing lasting would come of it. There would be no relief from her tired routine. She'd soon have to return home to Rosemary Run and her perpetually exhausting job as a pediatric nurse. The thought of wearing frumpy scrubs all day with her hair pulled back in an unimaginative bun while patients flung bodily fluids had been the last thing she'd wanted to focus on, yet the reality had forced its way to the forefront of her mind. No more glam outfits or sexy strangers to appreciate them. Her flight would leave in less than twenty-four hours.

Amelia sighed heavily as she sipped a cocktail at the hotel bar, absentmindedly stirring the festive, colored liquid and watching it slosh in her glass. She was itching for something. She couldn't quite wrap her mind around what or put words to the emotions that coursed through her, but she felt the discontent deep in her bones. She had hoped that her time in Vegas would make things better. She'd dreamed of divine intervention. Or something of the sort. Luck, maybe. Serendipity. She'd wished for the kind of self discovery Elizabeth Gilbert wrote about in *Eat Pray Love* or the kind Cheryl Strayed found on the Pacific Coast Trail as described in *Wild*. The kind that is almost forced upon a person, if they just show up and remain open to whatever the Universe wants to dish their way.

Now time was running short and nothing, it seemed, would turn out like she'd hoped. Soon, Amelia would have to admit to herself that the trip was a bust. Nothing life-changing had happened. Not really.

And then, a breath of fresh air on a sad, tired day, he walked in.

If Amelia had known the havoc this man would wreak in her life, maybe she would have ignored him and walked away. She *should* have walked away. In fact, she should have run away. She should have thrown cash down on the bar to pay for her drink, then slinked out the back before he could notice her. She should have returned to her hotel room and packed her bags alongside Rebecca. She should have blocked out everything except getting on the airplane and flying home.

Unfortunately, she did none of those things. Against her better judgement, she let herself fall into depths the likes of which she had never seen before.

1

"He wants me to go away with him," Amelia said to Rebecca as they lounged on the cushy blue sofa together in the stylishly-decorated Tatum home.

James was at work, but both Amelia and Rebecca had the day off. They planned to spend their free time watching trash TV and ordering takeout for lunch. It was to be a much needed reprieve from their busy schedules. Something about taking a day off in the middle of the week felt extra luxurious. Like playing hooky from school as a kid. They had discussed their plans for the day, and the only thing left to decide was whether to order Chinese food from a new restaurant on the outskirts of town or to have Garfield's Pizza-- an old favorite-- delivered.

Amelia had come straight from an overnight shift at the region's hospital in the neighboring town of Sweet

Balm Bay and was too tired to do anything but plop down next to her friend and veg out. Berryhill Community Medical Center was a good employer, but working as a nurse meant long hours on her feet with little time to recover. Amelia came off of each shift thoroughly exhausted. But she wanted to spend the day with Rebecca, so she pushed through her fatigue and drowsiness. She would likely doze on and off during breaks in the conversation. Rebecca would understand. She always did.

Rebecca had high standards for herself, but she didn't judge her friends or extended family members against the same benchmarks. Especially not her closest friends, like Amelia. When it came to Amelia, Rebecca endeavored to be understanding and gentle. Rebecca knew full well that Amelia needed a soft touch. She figured that the world was cruel enough. She wanted to be a soft place for her friend to fall.

Amelia made her announcement matter-of-factly, as if she had no apprehension about being alone with the man. He was her husband, after all. She was alone with him on a regular basis in the apartment they shared, but there, her friends and family were just a phone call away. Not to mention, the good folks at the Rosemary Run Police Department were on duty, ready to intervene should things turn ugly.

This was different. He wanted to take her into the woods, off the grid.

It was a sad state of affairs for a woman to be afraid of her own husband, yet that's where Amelia found herself. She hadn't yet admitted it to anyone else. She had barely admitted it to herself, instead pushing the fear away when it crept into her conscious thoughts. It was easier to pretend that things weren't so bad than to face what was happening. Amelia knew that she had chosen to marry him. Her friends and family members had urged her to wait and get to know him better before tying the knot. They would say they'd told her so. She couldn't bear hearing it from them. Not now. Maybe not ever.

Rebecca pursed her lips and tucked strands of her long red hair behind one ear. She felt sorry for her friend, but had warned her back when there was plenty of time to change course. She couldn't help but wonder how often she should keep gently repeating herself to Amelia when it didn't seem to do any good. At what point did gentle treatment become enabling? It seemed to be a fine line, one that was sometimes hard to navigate.

Rebecca had felt the same way when her brother-in-law, Mick, was killed and her sister-in-law, Cate, hopped into bed shortly afterward with one of the detectives investigating Mick's murder. To be fair, that had turned out surprisingly well. Cate and Neil were still together, in love and going strong. Rebecca supposed that crazy situations sometimes ended up good. Even so, she hesitated, hoping the subject would change to something more pleasant.

"What do you think?" Amelia asked, genuinely interested in Rebecca's opinion. "Should I go? Tell me the truth, Bec."

"Oh, I don't know," Rebecca replied. She considered how to best steer the conversation away from the matter at hand. She'd prefer not to discuss Amelia's relationship issues. And Amelia had big relationship issues, whether she realized it or not. "I'm still surprised he moved here in the first place. It's a big change for him. How do you think he's adjusting?"

Amelia pressed her head against a throw pillow and narrowed her eyes. "I see what you did there," she said with a chuckle. She wasn't mad, but she intended to get a straight answer from her friend. "You aren't fooling me with your tricks."

Rebecca smiled, then sighed.

"I'll say it again. Tell me the truth," Amelia prompted. "I count on you, you know. You're my best friend. I need you to keep me on the straight and narrow. To be my moral compass, and all that jazz."

"I do," Rebecca said. "But let's be honest. We both know there are parts of your life that you don't share with me. At least, not completely. It's been that way for as long as I can remember."

She was right. There had been many times during their decades-long friendship that Amelia had done certain things without telling Rebecca. Those things had typically involved risky sexual behavior and questionable choices about boyfriends. The chasm between them had only widened over the years when it came to this topic. From the perspective of an outsider looking in, it might have been hard to imagine how the women remained close given such a difference in values.

Ever since the pair had met in Freshman English class at the University of Nevada in Las Vegas, their philosophy on relationships and boys was the only thing they didn't see eye-to-eye on. Rebecca had been careful, never kissing on the first date and certainly never getting into bed with someone until they were in a long-term, committed relationship. She'd had only three serious boyfriends during her college years, the last one being James, who later became her husband. Rebecca's approach to dating was measured. She took her time, making sure that the men she became involved with were worthy of her trust. She had lost out on a few opportunities because of her serious approach to dating, but she didn't mind. Rebecca was far more interested in quality than quantity.

Not so for Amelia, which Rebecca had always found somewhat odd, given Amelia's seriousness when it came to matters of academics and later, her career. Amelia never missed a class, and she graduated from UNLV with top honors. She passed her nursing exams with flying colors. When the friends returned home to Rosemary Run-- Rebecca a native and Amelia a new resident having moved to live near her best friend-- and settled into their careers, Amelia had excelled in her job. She'd been promoted several times and had risen to the top of her group at the hospital. Amelia's career as a nurse had kept pace with Rebecca's career as an accountant. Both women were well liked and respected professionally. Why, then, had Amelia's smarts about romantic relationships lagged so far behind?

Amelia shifted uncomfortably on the sofa, clearly thrown off by her friend's mention of the things she'd kept hidden. It was an unusually direct statement coming from Rebecca. Especially on this topic. It reminded Amelia of Rebecca's stern warning when she'd told her she was getting married after just three months of dating her new beau.

"What do you mean?" Amelia asked, even though she knew exactly what Rebecca meant.

"Are you going to make me spell it out?" Rebecca asked. "Please, don't. You know I love you, Amelia. I only want what's best."

"What I know is that you don't like him," Amelia hissed. "You never even gave him a chance."

"That's not fair," Rebecca replied. "I've given him a chance, believe me."

"Just because he isn't a goody-goody boy scout like James doesn't mean he's trash."

"Come, now. Trash is a harsh word. I'd never say that about him," Rebecca replied, her tone even. She wasn't prone to dramatics, and she rarely allowed herself to get riled.

Amelia sat up and moved to the edge of her seat. She knew she needed to shift the mood between them. "Hey," she began. "How about I make us a drink? A little alcohol might be just what the doctor ordered."

Rebecca grimaced. She wasn't much of a drinker. She rarely drank more than once or twice a week, and almost never this early in the day.

"Oh, don't give me that face," Amelia scolded. "Come on. It will loosen things up. How about something simple. Wine? Do you have a bottle?"

Nearly everyone in Rosemary Run had a bottle of wine on hand at any given time. The region was known far and wide for the delicious wine produced locally. Keeping some on hand was almost obligatory. If nothing else, it came in handy when entertaining guests.

"I don't," Rebecca replied.

"Seriously?"

"Seriously. James and I aren't big drinkers. You know that."

A look of disappointment settled over Amelia's face. She was trying to talk to Rebecca about an important matter, and she needed a way to ease into it. She had decisions to make. Hard ones. Amelia had the distinct sense that her future would be decided during today's conversation with her friend. She knew that Rebecca would probably be surprised to learn the details of her dysfunctional romantic life. But she had to tell her anyway, before it was too late. Someone should know before she went off grid.

"Okay, then," Amelia said. "Since you don't have wine here, let's go out somewhere and have wine with lunch."

"Oh, I don't know," Rebecca replied too quickly. "I thought we were staying in today. Aren't you tired after working all night?"

Amelia pulled her shirt away from her chest, then leaned down and stuck her nose inside, smelling for body odor. It was a crude gesture, but one that was typical for Amelia when in Rebecca's company. It was striking how comfortable Amelia was around Rebecca in most regards. Yet, telling her the truth about her relationship with her new husband felt like a very hard thing to do. The irony wasn't lost on either of them.

"If you'd be so kind as to let me take a quick shower and borrow some of your clothes, I'll be good as new," Amelia said.

Rebecca didn't mind any of that, and Amelia knew it. But she could tell that Amelia had something unpleasant to discuss when they got wherever they were going. As the wife of a cop, Rebecca had developed a sixth sense about that kind of thing. And not just with Amelia. For better or worse, James' job had made them both skeptical and a bit paranoid, always waiting for the other shoe to drop.

"Where do you want to go?" Rebecca asked.

Amelia already had a place in mind. "Maison du Vin," she suggested. "I hear that the owner, Marcheline Fay, opened up a new restaurant on the property. I've been dying to try it."

"Really?" Rebecca asked. "I knew about the bakery her parents opened in town, but I hadn't heard about a restaurant at the vineyard."

Rebecca had always loved the beauty of Rosemary Run's local vineyards, and Maison du Vin was one of the prettiest of all. Eating outside with a view of the vineyard sounded appealing.

"Come on, Bec," Amelia said. "I know how you love the vineyards. It'll be nice. Just the two of us, drinking wine and eating whatever deliciousness Marcheline serves up. I hear the restaurant is a joint venture with the French guy she recently married. Julien somebody or another."

"Ah, right," Rebecca confirmed. "Julien Caron. Those two sound like a match made in heaven." She instantly regretted saying so. It was callous of her to make comments about happy couples when she knew Amelia was struggling. "I'm sorry," she added. "I didn't mean…"

"Stop it," Amelia said. "I know."

The friends looked at each other. They didn't need words to communicate. Rebecca knew that Amelia needed her. And she knew that time was of the essence.

"Okay," Rebecca said. "Go upstairs to get showered and changed. Pick out anything you want to wear from my closet. I'll use the guest bathroom to spruce myself up a bit, then I'll call us a car."

Amelia leaped up, practically shrieking with excitement. "Thank you, Bec. It'll be fun. You'll see." She bounded up the stairs to get ready, humming the tune to Stayin' Alive by the Bee Gees. She slowed every few steps to dance along with the beat.

Rebecca smiled back, appreciating Amelia's sense of humor while, at the same time, steeling herself for whatever bomb her friend was preparing to drop over lunch. She told herself to stay positive, but she had a terrible, sinking feeling. She was concerned for Amelia. And she was aware of the obligation to look out for her. If Amelia's new husband was a legitimate threat, Rebecca would have no choice but to get James involved.

Rebecca closed her eyes, breathing deeply and hoping that things weren't as treacherous as they seemed. "Oh, Amelia, my dear, dear, friend," Rebecca muttered to herself as she clasped her hands together in front of her chest. "I hope to God we can save you."

2

———

A Year Prior, Back Then
Las Vegas, Nevada

Amelia heard someone at the other end of the bar call out his name as he made his way into the room. Soon, a chorus of others chimed in. *Michael Bell.* It had a nice ring to it.

The hubbub from the bar patrons reminded her of an old sitcom called *Cheer's* that her parents had always raved about. She'd seen the reruns, thanks to her mom's long-standing crush on Ted Danson and the Sam Malone character he played on the show. Amelia remembered how one of the other characters, named Norm, was greeted with a cheerful shout of his name every time he walked in the door of the Boston-area bar the series was centered around.

Was Michael Bell that much of a regular here, in this Las Vegas hotel bar? Was he that well loved and admired? If so, he sounded like just the kind of man Amelia was looking for. She let her mind wander, quickly sizing Michael up and speculating about his personal life. If he was known here, she figured it must mean that he lived in the area. Or-- at minimum-- that he visited often. The idea was appealing. Dating someone with a Vegas connection seemed fun and adventurous. She had enjoyed her college years in the area. And now, she desperately needed to extend the fun and adventure in her life. A tie to her college days seemed like the perfect way to do it.

Amelia's back straightened as Michael walked toward her. Her entire body went on high alert. She chewed her lip, seemingly unable to help herself. Goosebumps covered her skin, and the hair on the back of her neck stood up. Whether her physical reaction was a sign of good things or a warning of trouble to come, she didn't know. Should she run towards this mystery man? Or away from him? All she did know was that Michael Bell was impossible to ignore. Something was happening to her. Something was happening to *them*.

She couldn't ignore it. She didn't want to.

Michael was unusually tall and handsome, with dirty blonde hair cropped close against his head and brilliant green eyes that seemed to pierce the very air around them. His motions were smooth, like those of a tiger. He was built strong and muscular like a wild animal, his body full of latent energy. He wore fitted jeans and a black shirt underneath a tailored sport coat that was in perfect condition. His clothes appeared to be new, and they weren't cheap. Each item, down to his white sneakers, was perfectly suited to his distinct sense of style.

Amelia felt a pang of self-consciousness. She swiped at

her black halter top, adjusting the low neckline around her perky cleavage. It hung cooperatively, skimming her hips and the tight-fitting jeans that extended down her long legs and gripped her shapely ankles. The outfit was new-- purchased a few days prior-- but Amelia suddenly wished she'd been wearing something even more seductive. She silently scolded herself for not paying closer attention to her appearance. She knew she looked good, but she wanted to look her very best. Keeping herself in tip-top condition all week had been a priority. She hated that she had let things slip a bit on the day that this sultry man walked into her life. She thought she could have made a better impression wearing a dress, with heavier makeup and higher heels.

Michael's charisma was off the charts. At least, Amelia thought so. The way he moved, the way he smiled, and the drawl in his voice piqued her interest. She instantly understood that Michael Bell was different than any man she'd ever known. She wanted to find out more about him. She wanted to find a way to keep him in her life. It was a lot to decide about a person at first sight, but she had. Her decisions were made quickly, and at a deep level. No one could have changed her mind if they'd tried.

He was drawn to her, too.

Michael's eyes stopped on Amelia's as he scanned the room. For a moment in time, everything else faded and became distant as the pair gazed at each other, taking each other in. She looked at his mouth, tracing the lines of his lips into her memory so she could recall them later. He surveyed her figure, following her curves down to her manicured toes, then back up again. The attraction between them was undeniable. It was obvious to everyone in the room. Heads began to turn as people felt the electricity between these star-crossed lovers. It was as if they were predestined to meet like this, and those in their company could feel it, even though Amelia and Michael had not yet made each other's acquaintance. Not officially. But it seemed like they'd known each other forever.

Maybe it was a test of Amelia's judgement. An opportunity for her to make choices in her own best interest rather than give in to short-sighted temptation and hollow connections.

A wiser woman would have known that animal magnetism is very different from real, sustainable love. It sometimes happens together, but not in this case. There were clues that pointed to the danger surrounding Michael, had Amelia been savvy enough to see them. A wiser woman would have seen through Michael's swagger enough to question the response from the crowd and the posse that followed him. She would have seen the ridiculously expensive watch on his arm, the wads of cash bulging from his pockets, and the way people looked at him for approval.

Rebecca would have seen the clues. Had she been at the bar, she would have, at least, tried to prevent her friend from making the biggest mistake of her life. Someone should have. Yet Amelia was there all alone, without anyone to save her. She was unattended. In many ways, she was a hurt child in adult form, completely unequipped to protect herself from dangerous men like Michael.

Maybe the gods were watching. Maybe Amelia's very fate hung in the balance.

As it turned out, this was one of many junctures where Amelia could have taken a different path and in doing so, saved herself from suffering. She didn't seem to realize the importance of what was happening. At least, not consciously. She was acting on impulse borne from old hurts.

"Hello, ma'am," Michael said slowly, nodding his head politely as he crossed in front of Amelia and made his way to a high-top table at the back of the room.

His accent sounded Southern. Amelia's imagination went into overdrive, thinking of how that Southern drawl would sound whispered into her ear. She wanted more than anything to be truly and deeply loved by a man. To be desired sexually, but even more so to be cherished and taken care of.

Ever since she was a little girl, Amelia had dreamed of her wedding day. She had envisioned herself in a flowing white gown that accentuated all of her best features, in a classy way. She knew the exact kind of veil she'd wear, and she had picked out a blue corset to wear for the event. It would fit the bill for the "something blue" that was part of the old-time tradition, along with somethings old, new, and borrowed. To say Amelia was dedicated to making her dreams come true would be an understatement. Especially now that she was getting older and her biological clock was ticking. She was hyper focused on becoming a Mrs.

A trio of men followed Michael and sat down, although Amelia scarcely noticed them. They blended into the background, the same as the paneling on the walls and the waiters and waitresses darting in and out of the room.

Her gaze was fixed on Michael. When he looked her way and winked, she knew she had to talk to him. It was now or never. The opportunity was right in front of her. This could be her chance. This could be her man. He could be her future. Her everything.

Amelia stood, her legs feeling wobbly beneath her. She pushed her cocktail glass away from the edge of the bar clumsily. It should have been an easy, smooth motion, but it wasn't. It felt like the ground was moving beneath her and that everything was unstable. For a split second, she wondered if an earthquake was happening. Except that she knew it wasn't because everyone else in the room seemed to be on stable footing.

Amelia had been a soccer player in college and was usually graceful and agile on her feet, but the ball of nerves in her stomach seemed to be making her limbs short circuit. She wished Rebecca were there to give her a hand, although she knew Rebecca had no place in this encounter. Amelia was on her own.

She glanced back at Michael, then took a step forward, one hand reaching out for the empty stool next to her in an effort to steady herself. Only, the stool wasn't as close as she had expected. Suddenly thrown off balance, Amelia lost her footing and tumbled head first onto the floor. Her feet moved in counterbalance, flying into the air above her. It was a dramatic fall that felt to Amelia like it went against the laws of physics. She had never in life fallen like this. What auspicious timing. She knew Michael was witnessing the whole thing.

When she landed in a heap against the alcohol-stained carpet, the only thing Amelia could think was that it was good she hadn't worn a dress after all. She was mortified. And hurt. She had twisted her wrist on the way down. Being a nurse, she knew immediately that it might be sprained. She would need to get it looked at by a medical professional.

"I'm okay!" Amelia shouted, to no one in particular.

She could feel her face turning red with embarrassment. The crowd was stunned, unsure of what to say or do. No one moved to help her. There was an awkward silence. Someone turned off the music, which only made the situation worse. Every single person in the room was staring at her. Those eating had even stopped chewing their food, their mouths hanging open as they stared at the spectacle unfolding in front of them.

Amelia wanted to crawl on her hands and knees across the floor and get out of there. No matter how much she wanted to talk to Michael, she hadn't wanted it to happen like this. Tears forced themselves from her eyes and she began to cry. The situation was excruciatingly uncomfortable. It didn't seem like it could get any worse.

The same way Michael had startled Amelia when he walked in the door, he did it again as his face appeared next to hers. He seemed to show up from out of nowhere. She hadn't heard him walking towards her. He was just there. Ashamed, yet eager for his attention, she looked up at him.

"Michael Bell?" she asked.

Amelia's voice was soft and timid. She hated that it was coming out that way-- like the voice of a child instead of a grown woman. Michael smiled broadly, apparently finding her amusing. Or endearing. She couldn't tell which.

"Who's asking?" he replied in his slow drawl.

His voice sent a shiver up and down her spine. But she was tongue tied, unable to form words to speak to the man, even though she desperately wanted to. When she didn't reply right away, he extended his hand toward her. Using her uninjured hand, she took his and allowed him to help her up. She cradled her hurt wrist against her chest, protecting it as she got to her feet.

"I'm Amelia," she finally said. "Amelia Baker."

"Pleased to meet you, Amelia Baker," he replied. "How do you know my name, anyway?"

She shuffled onto the barstool she had occupied before, careful to move deliberately so as to avoid another spill.

"I heard people saying it when you walked in," she explained.

"Good," he said. "Now that you know who I am, I hope you'll let me take care of you."

3

———

Present Day
Rosemary Run, California

Amelia and Rebecca chatted happily as they rode in the back of the zippy black sports car that had arrived to take them to Maison du Vin. Their driver was a woman in her golden years who told them she had retired from her corporate job in Sacramento and moved to Rosemary Run to work part time in the area's booming tourism industry. Her name was Glada. She was so pleasant, that Rebecca considered inviting her to lunch. They didn't, but they asked for her contact information so they could request her the next time they hired a rideshare service.

Glada's upbeat vibe and positive attitude energized Amelia and Rebecca. It reminded them of the excitement they'd felt on the way to Las Vegas the year prior. They'd had such high expectations for the trip. From Amelia's point of view-- at least, the one she told herself-- it had been a roaring success. She had met Michael and fallen head over heels in a passionate love affair for the ages. Rebecca didn't feel the same. Quite the opposite, actually. She now considered that trip one of the worst turns in her friend's life. And Amelia's troubles affected Rebecca, too.

"Do you feel that?" Amelia asked her friend as they stepped out of Glada's car into the warm sunshine and gentle, cool breeze.

It was early November, and the weather in Rosemary Run was what Amelia considered to be near perfection. It rarely snowed at the lower elevations where the town was located, but leaves changed and temperatures dipped around this time every year. The turn of the seasons brought an energy all its own that most of the locals looked forward to.

Both ladies were dressed in stylish boots, curve-hugging jeans, and jewel-toned sweaters. They carried leather handbags in coordinating shades of brown. They looked like the picture of genuine happiness and fulfilling friendship. They were gorgeous women, each in their own right. They could have easily been featured in Vine Country Magazine, the region's glossy lifestyle publication.

"What?" Rebecca asked, working towards a smile. She was trying to remain positive.

"The good vibes or juju or whatever you want to call it," Amelia replied. "Something good is about to happen. I can feel it."

Rebecca grimaced. She couldn't help herself. She was beginning to think that Amelia's instincts had gone haywire. She didn't imagine anything good coming next.

In fact, her own gut told her that danger lurked very near. She tried her best to push the feeling down. They were having lunch together at a picturesque vineyard on a beautiful day, after all. What could go wrong?

"If you say so," Rebecca replied, forcing the corners of her lips sideways to feign a smile.

Amelia could tell that her friend was bothered, but she forged on. "Hey," she said as she waved goodbye to Glada, then set her handbag on a bench nearby. "Let's take a selfie. Right here, with the vineyard and the Maison du Vin sign behind us. I want to remember this day."

Rebecca liked the idea. She hated to even think it, but deep down, she feared that Amelia wouldn't always be around. She wanted to remember her as she was. Rebecca nodded her approval as Amelia pulled her smartphone out of her back pocket, turned the camera on, and positioned it out in front of them at just the right angle. They leaned their heads together at the temples and posed.

"Smile!" Amelia said cheerfully, poking her friend playfully in the side. "Like you mean it."

Rebecca chuckled. Amelia had a way of making her laugh, even during difficult times. It was one of the many reasons she loved her.

"Fine," Rebecca said, loosening up a little. "Cheese!"

Amelia snapped a series of photos, adjusting the camera settings and angles of the shot each time. When Rebecca protested at the number of snaps, Amelia asked for just a few more.

"I told you, Bec," Amelia said. "I want to remember this day. Besides, you're my best friend. We should take more pictures of the two of us together."

Suddenly uncomfortable with the serious tone, Rebecca backed away, her face drooping. Before she knew it, a tear had formed in her eye. She turned from her friend, wiping it away quickly in the hopes that Amelia wouldn't notice. The swift back and forth motion of her hand reminded her of the way mothers wiped tears from their toddlers' eyes. Rebecca wished someone were here to help her keep it together. Someone besides Amelia.

"I'm sorry," Rebecca said. "I don't know what's come over me."

Amelia put the phone back in her pocket and placed an arm around her friend. "Hey, now, it's okay, Bec. What's going on?"

Amelia knew full well what was going on, but didn't want to say it.

"It's nothing," Rebecca said. "Don't worry about it. I'm fine."

"Except that you aren't," Amelia said.

Rebecca shrugged. More tears forced their way out and streamed down her cheeks, against her will. She wiped them away. Then she sighed slowly, exhaling air she hadn't even realized she'd been holding. Shouldn't Amelia be the one upset? Rebecca silently scolded herself for being such an empath. She cared too much. If Amelia couldn't realize what a mess her life had become and take action to do something about it, why should Rebecca let herself get so worked up over it? Yet, she couldn't seem to help herself.

"I really am sorry, Amelia," Rebecca said. "I want to support you. I do. I've tried to put on a brave face and let you make your own decisions. I don't want to bring you down or dampen your happiness… You're a new bride…"

Amelia's shoulders slumped. "You're talking about Michael, aren't you? You want to bash my husband."

Rebecca nodded. "I don't mean to *bash* him, but isn't he what you brought me here to discuss?"

Amelia shook her head, growing visibly upset. Her brow furrowed and her cheeks turned nearly as red as her sweater. "No. Well, I don't know. Maybe."

"Which is it?" Rebecca asked. "Ever since you and Troy broke up last year, I've felt like I was walking on eggshells every time the topic of your love life comes up. It isn't fair. It makes things between us… well, strained, to say the least."

Amelia looked at the ground, defeated. Troy Weeks had been a gaffe, or so she'd thought at the time. He was too ordinary. Too even keel. Too stable. When they'd broken up, she'd dated a string of men who might have replaced Troy and drowned out those memories. None had done the job, which is why she and Rebecca had booked the last minute trip to Vegas in search of excitement. She had certainly found it in Michael, but she was beginning to think it wasn't what was best for her, after all. She was beginning to think that *Michael* wasn't what was best for her.

"Why do you have to bring Troy up?" Amelia asked. "I don't even want to hear his name, Bec. I'd like to leave him in my rearview mirror," she lied, to both Rebecca and to herself.

"Because he was a genuinely good guy, Amelia. I hate that the two of you didn't end up together. I always hoped you would. The two of you would have made the most beautiful mixed babies. His strong, dark features and broad build along with your smooth skin and delicate frame would have been such a winning combination."

"Stop it," Amelia whispered under her breath.

She had thought the same thing herself. Her Italian heritage and Troy's African heritage had seemed like a good combination when it came to baby making.

"Don't pretend you didn't think about having kids with him," Rebecca said. "He'd make an amazing dad. That's obvious to everyone who knows him."

Amelia and Troy had talked about being together forever. In fact, Troy had proposed. Rebecca didn't know that part. It was a sore subject for Amelia. She'd walked away from Troy's proposal-- literally-- leaving him on one knee in their backyard as she jumped in her car and sped away. They had lived together for nearly three years, but Amelia freaked out at the reality of an engagement.

"What do you know about baby making, anyway?" Amelia snapped.

It was a cruel question. Rebecca and James didn't have kids, despite being well into their thirties. Amelia knew they wanted to have babies of their own someday, and that it hadn't happened naturally yet. The couple had recently set a timeline. If Rebecca didn't become pregnant within the next year and a half, they'd enlist the help of a fertility specialist.

"Really?" Rebecca asked. "You went there."

An older couple parked their car nearby, then walked past Amelia and Rebecca on their way into Maison du Vin. They were all smiles, apparently there for lunch as well. The friends stayed quiet while they waited on the old folks to go by. The pause was needed. It helped to lower the level of tension, if only a bit. By the time the old couple reached the front door and disappeared inside, the discussion that had been careening towards a nasty dispute between friends had softened. The two of them had already learned that it was a bad idea to talk about Amelia's husband, especially when his name was mentioned directly. It sent things into a downward spiral, every time, without fail. The topic of Amelia's volatile marriage required delicate treatment.

"Let's try this again," Amelia said. "We should start over. I didn't mean to hurt your feelings, Bec… You know, about the babies. You and James will have them. I know you will."

"Agreed," Rebecca replied. "Forget all of that. Moving on. Let's get inside and have a nice lunch before you tell me whatever it is you want to share."

"Yeah, we can talk after we have a few drinks in us. That ought to help," Amelia suggested.

Even though Rebecca wasn't much of a drinker, she thought her friend might be right. A few drinks might be exactly what was needed at this juncture. The pair hugged each other tightly, a gesture of peace. Then they walked inside the restaurant arm in arm. Their friendship was too important to them both to let anything come in between them. How they would navigate the troubled waters ahead was another matter that they'd tackle as best they could. One step at a time.

When they arrived at the hostess stand in the lobby of the charming new restaurant, they were greeted by a friendly young woman named Leigh who sat them at a table on the second-story deck next to an open window. Leigh was every bit as chipper and bright as Glada had been. Amelia and Rebecca appreciated her enthusiasm and hoped that the positive vibes from the strangers they'd met that day were a good sign. They needed all the positivity they could get.

Leigh told them she'd be their waitress and presented them with a lengthy wine list and an extensive lunch menu of tasty French faire. They ordered a bottle of red wine and an appetizer made of goat cheese and tart apple on French bread. It sounded dreamy, and when it arrived a short time later, it tasted every bit as good as it sounded.

"My God," Amelia blurted as she chewed. "This is heavenly. Almost better than sex."

Rebecca blushed, glancing around to see if anyone overheard her friend's comment. The lunch rush was in full swing by this time and the dining room was packed. Of course, several people had overhead and looked their way. Amelia didn't care. She wasn't usually concerned about decorum. Not really.

"Amelia, shush," Rebecca whispered, leaning low over the table.

"What?" Amelia asked. "Chill, Bec. I guarantee you everyone in this room has had sex before. I'm just saying what everyone else is thinking. Everyone who tasted this amazing food, anyway."

Before Rebecca could respond, her attention was drawn to a commotion at the hostess stand. She craned her neck and could see Leigh, her body language distressed. She was being harassed by a man who spoke far too loudly. He was waving his arms and pointing his finger in Leigh's face. Rebecca couldn't see him around the large column obscuring her view, but she thought she recognized his voice. Amelia recognized it, too, and she locked eyes with her friend. Amelia didn't turn to identify the man. She already knew.

"Michael," Amelia said, his name practically sticking in her throat. "He's here to take me away."

4

———

A Year Prior, Back Then
Las Vegas, Nevada

It had been just a few short hours since Michael had picked Amelia up off the floor after her fall. He had charmed her with a strong, steady hand and a string of compliments, then he'd taken her to his penthouse overlooking the famous Las Vegas strip for another stiff drink. She hadn't objected.

Amelia had been under Michael's spell since the moment she laid eyes on him. He could have asked her for anything-- to *do* anything-- and she would have happily obliged. In fact, he had already asked her to extend her stay in Nevada so they could spend time together, and she had done just that. She had cancelled her flight home to California, sending text messages to both her boss and Rebecca to say simply that something had come up. She hadn't bothered to elaborate. She had known they'd both be upset, but she didn't care. She would have quit her job if Michael had asked her to. She knew it was crazy, but she didn't care about that, either.

"How's your drink?" Michael asked as smooth jazz played in the background and lights glimmered on the balcony. The sun was beginning to retreat for the day and the artificial lights outside created a sultry, romantic ambiance.

Amelia was already buzzed. Michael had made her a black Russian with 100-proof vodka, coffee liqueur, and a maraschino cherry. She didn't think she'd had such a strong drink before, but she hadn't wanted to mention it and appear unsophisticated. When Michael handed her the glass, she had nodded politely and taken it from him with a smile, eager to please.

Michael understood the power he had over Amelia. He knew what it meant to take advantage of a vulnerable woman. He'd done it before, and he wouldn't hesitate to do it again. Especially not when he needed something that woman could provide. He had big plans for Amelia Baker. He'd been waiting for the right woman to show up. He was as happy to make her acquaintance as she was his, only for different reasons.

"It's good," Amelia said, her words beginning to slur. "A little strong, but good. I like it."

"Too much for you?" he asked, winking.

"I didn't say that," she replied.

"Then you're ready for another one?"

Amelia hesitated for a split second, but couldn't bring herself to disappoint this sexy, powerful, hunk of a man. She wanted to make him happy.

"Sure," she said, tossing back the remaining liquid in

her glass and then holding it out for more. "If you insist. Fill 'er up. As long as you're taking care of me tonight."

He'd said those words, and she clung to them.

"I'm taking care of you, alright," he confirmed. "Relax. I've got you."

Michael took the glass from Amelia and returned to his mini-bar to make her a second drink. He didn't take his eyes off of her as he moved. She found his attentiveness extremely alluring. She practically glowed under the admiration and affection he was showering on her. He had said all the right things, and he was making all the right moves.

Amelia had already decided to have sex with Michael if the chance presented itself, but she'd also already decided she wanted more. She felt differently about him than she had the city slicker, the motorcycle dude, or the female performer. Those had been distractions. This could be something real. Or so she told herself. This could be what she'd been waiting for.

Amelia hadn't noticed, but Michael hadn't been drinking. He had sipped water from a glass under the bar every once in a while, but he hadn't ingested any alcohol. A wiser woman would have noticed.

Her head began to spin as she sat on the plush gray sofa and waited for Michael to return. She had a flash of doubt, wondering if he might have slipped something into her drink. A drug, she speculated. Like a date-rape drug. *Surely not*, she thought. She pushed the thought out of her mind as fast as it had entered. Michael seemed to her like a nice guy. A good guy. Surely, he wouldn't harm her. She figured that's the stuff of dramatic movies and television. Not real life. Not *her* real life.

Amelia squinted her eyes as she tried her best to remain lucid. She had been drinking when they'd met, and had imbibed more today than any other day she could remember. She was beyond any known bounds. She wasn't sure what to do about it.

"Here you go," Michael said, suddenly in front of her and handing her drink number two. "Enjoy it, my dear."

Amelia blushed at the term. Being called dear struck her as old-fashioned, yet it sounded sexy in Michael's Southern accent. She felt a rush of warmth and pressure between her legs. She wanted him. And she wanted him now. Feeling a surge of confidence, Amelia leaned forward, going in for a kiss. Only, her balance was off and she nearly headbutted Michael square in the nose. Embarrassed, she retreated backward and downed some of the mixed drink nervously.

"Sorry," she mumbled.

It wasn't like her to be so nervous and clumsy around a man. What had gotten into her? She honestly didn't know. At least, that's what she told herself.

"Don't worry about it," Michael said, gently guiding the glass with his hand and urging her to keep drinking. A wiser woman would have noticed that he seemed to be trying to get her drunk. It was subtle, but it was there, happening nonetheless.

"You probably think I'm a clutz," Amelia said, cradling the wrist she'd injured in her fall at the bar earlier that day.

She had practically forgotten about it. There had been

too much on her mind. She hadn't even told Michael how much it hurt. She'd suspected the alcohol had something to do with her ability to withstand the pain. She'd learned in nursing school that alcohol can numb both physical and emotional pain, sometimes leading patients to wait too long to seek treatment from a healthcare professional. Right now, she didn't care about that either. She told herself she'd tend to it later.

"Aren't we all?" Michael asked, putting her at ease.

He was good at putting her at ease. Too good.

A wiser woman would have noticed that someone else had entered the penthouse. But Amelia was losing what was left of her grip on reality as the moments wore on. Her vision was blurry now, and there was an incessant ringing in her ears that wouldn't stop. A wiser woman would have stood and gotten herself out of there. Amelia should have stood and gotten herself out of there. She should have run away, as fast as she could go. She should have called Rebecca. Or 9-1-1.

She heard a door slam somewhere in the distance.

"Michael?" she asked.

He was gone from her view, and she couldn't quite orient herself in order to look around the penthouse for him. She tried to stand, but could tell she wasn't steady on her feet. When Michael didn't answer after what felt to Amelia like a long time, she tried again.

"Michael?" she yelled, her voice breaking as she tried to yell.

Heavy footsteps approached from behind until Amelia could make out the shape of a man's legs. The legs were wearing a suit, not jeans like Michael had been earlier.

Amelia tried to look up to see the face that was attached to these new, foreign legs, but her eyes failed her. Her eyelids forced themselves shut even though inside, she was terrified. Her mind raced and bogged down at the same time in a cruel mishmash.

She reached out a hand to touch the legs. As she did, she quickly realized that they didn't belong to Michael. They were much larger than his. These legs felt like tree trunks. Like they belonged to a professional wrestler or bodyguard. This man must have been huge.

Before Amelia could open her mouth to speak again, an enormous hand grabbed her by the throat and pulled her unceremoniously off the sofa. She thought she saw other figures in the background-- at least two more men-- but she couldn't get a good look at them before she lost consciousness and blacked out. Like it or not, she was completely and totally at their mercy.

5

___

Present Day
Rosemary Run, California

When Michael stopped shouting, a hush fell over the restaurant and you could have heard a pin drop. Amelia wanted to crawl under the table and curl up like a small child. Heat rushed to her face. Her hands trembled, clanking against her silverware despite her efforts to steady them. No one in the restaurant knew yet that the loud, angry man was there looking for her. But soon enough, they would.

Rebecca held steady, her posture straight and strong. She knew the voice belonged to Michael. Unlike Amelia, she wouldn't cower to an aggressive man. Rebecca might have been demure, but she had boundaries. And standards. She'd face Michael— and any other bully— head on. She picked up her phone to text James. Her husband should be here to keep the peace. He was a cop, after all. He would be out on patrol this time of day, anyway. He could swing by, probably able to arrive within minutes.

At Maison du Vin with A. Michael is here causing a disturbance. Looks like it will escalate. Help?

A whoosh sound rang out as the message was sent.

"What do you mean when you say he's here to take you away?" Rebecca asked. "That doesn't sound good, Amelia. None of this sounds good. Are you in trouble?"

"I... I don't know..."

Amelia had been afraid something like this would happen. The warning signs had been there. If only she'd listened to her gut— the deepest instinct that can't be overridden— instead of talking herself out of paying attention to the gnawing bad feelings that had haunted her since the day she met Michael. She had tried to manufacture good vibes. It had worked to an extent, but Michael's adversarial presence at Maison du Vin was proof that her efforts hadn't been enough.

Maybe a part of her had known to expect this public scene. Maybe bringing Rebecca out today was a cry for help. This disturbance wouldn't have been as dramatic if they'd stayed home at Rebecca's house. Except that maybe being in public lessened the danger.

"Get out of my way!" Michael shouted, shoving the hostess stand so hard that it went crashing to the floor with a bang.

Leigh shrieked and stumbled backward. From Amelia and Rebecca's vantage point, it didn't look like she was hit. She'd apparently retreated just in time. It concerned Rebecca that Michael had been willing to topple the wooden structure with Leigh so close to it. The young employee was clearly rattled. Her shoulders raised, and she wrapped her arms tightly around her torso as she watched in disbelief.

A low murmur erupted from the crowd as Michael tore around the column and stepped past the overturned hostess stand on his way to the dining room. A family with young children stood and scurried out the door. They didn't stop to pay their bill. The older couple who Amelia and Rebecca had seen walking in also stood and left, throwing cash on their table hastily, their salads only half eaten. By the looks of it, a slew of others were prepared to make their exit. Most of the Maison du Vin patrons didn't want to wait around and be part of drama. No one could blame them. Volatile men like Michael were dangerous. People with good sense tended to steer clear.

"He's coming," Amelia breathed, lifting one hand to shield her face from view. It was a feeble attempt to hide. Michael would recognize Amelia. She knew he would.

"Does he see us?" Rebecca asked calmly. She was careful to keep her wits about her. She didn't intend to show any signs of being fearful or intimidated.

"If he doesn't, he will soon enough."

"What are you going to do?" Rebecca asked her friend.

Amelia raised her brows, her face flush with embarrassment. "I'm going to apologize profusely to Marcheline Faye and her French husband for the disruption to their lunch service."

"Yeah, and before that?"

Michael sputtered and practically spit as he made his way through the dining room, searching the faces that remained. His anger was boiling. It was obvious he was seeing red, unable to be reasoned with. He muttered as he stomped, something unintelligible. No one dared to get in his way. Those who remained at their tables avoided his gaze as he passed them. He was like a bull in a china shop, knocking into chairs and snagging tablecloths. The worst part was, he was just getting started. He was still on the lowest level, but he was making his way toward the stairs that led to his wife's table. He'd be there in a matter of minutes. Amelia needed to decide what she was going to do, and fast.

"Bec, what should I do?" she asked. "Tell me. Quick! I'm in a bad spot here."

Rebecca shook her head, frustrated by the need to make this kind of decision. It wasn't hers to make. Yet Amelia was clearly unable to handle the situation on her own. And they were running out of time. Rebecca thought about Marcheline and the damage this scene would do to her business. She hated it. If it turned into a full blown domestic dispute, that would look even worse. Rebecca also thought about her text to James and how he'd hopefully be here soon. At this point, she figured other patrons would have called 9-1-1. James wouldn't be the only one showing up. Seeing no other choice, she made the decision to stall Michael in the hopes that she could buy her friend some time until help arrived.

"Get under the table," Rebecca instructed.

Her voice was flat, full of resignation. It hit Amelia's ears like a barb.

In an unusual flash of clarity, Amelia had a sense of the burden her bad choices were for her friends and family. Rebecca had shouldered the brunt of it, but she wasn't alone in wishing Amelia would gather her courage and remove Michael from her life. It was abundantly clear what needed done. At least, it was to everyone around her. For a brief moment in time, Amelia was beginning to see the truth. Better late than never. Only, it might be too late to get out unscathed.

The table was covered with a large white cloth that reached all the way to the floor. It would provide complete cover if Amelia hid underneath.

"What?" Amelia asked. "Are you serious?"

"Serious as a heart attack," Rebecca said. "Take your glass and place settings, too. Fast! Make it look like I'm dining alone."

Amelia appeared stunned, but she recovered quickly and followed her friend's instructions. She grabbed her plate with a remnant of the goat cheese appetizer, her glass of wine, her shiny silverware, and her cloth napkin, then dove beneath the table, tucking the cloth so she wouldn't be seen. She felt the eyes of strangers on her, but she ignored them. She had to prioritize her concerns. Right now, public opinion was not anywhere near the top of that list.

"Hurry!" Rebecca said as she smoothed the table cloth down with one hand. "He sees me."

She wasn't kidding. Michael had spotted her. He fumed as he trudged toward the table, his face a deep red. It was so red, Rebecca wondered if he was inebriated. He had the coloring of an addict who has trouble digesting the alcohol. Rebecca had seen the same look before. It scared her, although she willed herself to keep a strong presence. She wouldn't let on. If Michael sensed fear, it would only make him more aggressive.

"Where's my wife?" Michael shouted, his voice a loud roar as he reached the table.

"Hello, Michael," Rebecca said cooly.

He scoffed, frustrated with Rebecca's calm demeanor. Michael was a man who was used to getting what he wanted, especially from women. He didn't know what to make of Rebecca. He had tried to be cordial, but he didn't like her. The feeling was mutual.

"I asked you a question," he said, placing a fist down hard on the table. "Where is my wife?"

"Why are you asking me?" Rebecca asked.

Replying to a question with another question was a tried and true tactic to keep someone talking. Rebecca had learned it from James. It was one of the many tricks she'd picked up as the wife of a cop. She hoped it would work with Michael now. Every minute-- every second-- counted.

"Aren't you supposed to be her best friend?" he asked. "Surely, you know where she is."

"And you're her husband. I'd imagine that you know where she is. Didn't she tell you where she was going today?"

"Don't do that," he barked.

"Do what?"

Rebecca kept her cool, even as she felt Amelia shaking against her leg under the table.

"Don't patronize me," Michael replied. "I see what you're doing."

"What am I doing?"

Michael rared back, then brought both fists down on

the table with all of his strength. The table buckled under the pressure. It was wooden. Had it been made of flimsier material, it would have broken under the pressure. Michael was a strong man.

A child cried from somewhere in the background, and several more people scurried away through the exit doors. Rebecca didn't flinch. Out the corner of her eye, she thought she saw Marcheline directing employees in the kitchen. She didn't know Marcheline personally, but she'd seen her across the room a handful of times. She'd also seen her photograph in Vine Country Magazine. Rebecca wasn't sure what might be happening behind the scenes, but she was glad there was movement. Maybe someone knew what to do to put an end to this. Rebecca hoped whatever they were planning happened quickly, but she didn't allow Michael to get a rise out of her. She kept her face slack, her body language confident.

Michael took a deep breath, attempting to collect himself. It was little comfort to those in his presence. He was full of steam, like a teapot ready to blow its top.

"I know she's here because I tracked her phone," he explained. "You can stop pretending. You aren't eating lunch alone. Is she in the bathroom?"

Rebecca's face didn't divulge what she knew. She was a good friend, and she was doing a good job stalling Michael until help arrived. But it didn't matter. Amelia shuddered under the table, moving around nervously. Despite her efforts to remain quiet, Amelia's wedding ring clinked against a piece of the metal bracing beneath the table, alerting Michael to her presence.

"There she is," he said with a scowl. Then he leaned

down, lifted the tablecloth, and made eye contact with his terrified wife.

There was nothing left for Rebecca to do. She couldn't protect her friend physically. She could only say a silent prayer that someone would intervene. And fast.

6

A Year Prior, Back Then
Las Vegas, Nevada

When she came to, Amelia found herself in a soft, pillowy bed. She felt plush cushions beneath her aching body and squishy pillows under her throbbing head. Her responses were sluggish, and she was sore, as if she'd been run over by a truck. It took all of her energy to open her eyes and move ever so slightly under the silky covers. She winced when a searing pain shot through her jaw. It felt like someone was driving a nail right through the bone.

Pain was better than numbness. Better than nothingness.

Thank God, she thought. *I'm alive.*

It was an odd thing to think. Amelia hadn't consciously feared for her life before she blacked out, yet here she was, grateful to have survived the ordeal with

Michael and the thugs who had apparently taken her away from him.

Had they beaten her and left her for dead? Something must have happened to make her this sore. She'd sustained injuries. Even though Amelia couldn't immediately theorize how such a dramatic turn of events had happened, she thought maybe Michael had saved her. She figured that was the most likely thing to have happened. She couldn't fathom the possibility that Michael was a bad guy. No, from Amelia's distorted perspective, she believed him to be on her side. A man who would never harm her. In fact, she had begun to see Michael Bell as a hero. *Her* hero.

How wrong she was. How utterly, dangerously wrong.

Sun streamed in through a wall of windows as fluffy blue clouds floated by. It was mid-day, Amelia could discern that much for sure. She didn't know where she was, but she could tell she was high in the air. It seemed like she was amongst the clouds, sort of like the airplane that brought her to Las Vegas had been. She squinted against the sunlight. She'd need painkillers to ease her physical distress. She thought a drink or two might help as well.

Amelia didn't seem to know what was good for her physically, which was unusual for a nurse. For some reason, she was far better at taking care of others than she was at minding herself. Sometimes, it felt like a curse. Other times, she was convinced the proclivity made her look like a fraud.

Once, a few years prior, a minor cut from a jet ski accident had later become so infected that Amelia needed to check herself into the emergency room where several friends and colleagues worked. She had been terribly embarrassed. She had a habit of leaving her own cuts and scrapes unwashed even though she would have immediately cleaned and disinfected those of her patients. That memorable night in the ER as Amelia had ducked and dodged to keep people she knew from recognizing her, Rebecca had told Amelia in no uncertain terms: her behavior was bizarre. If only Rebecca were here now to knock some sense into her troubled friend.

"Hello?" Amelia asked, to no one in particular. Her voice shook. She didn't know whether she was alone, but she could have used a hand. "Is anyone there?"

Silence. The place was quiet except for the soft hum of the air conditioner.

"Michael?" she called, feebly.

No answer. She would have to do more to help herself.

Slowly, Amelia raised onto one elbow and peered into the long hallway just beyond the bedroom through an open door. The lighting in that direction was dim and her head pounded, but she thought the space around her was either a luxury hotel room or a swanky condo. The ceilings were high, and the finishings were luxurious. Was she still in Las Vegas? She couldn't be sure. The air felt dry, although it was hard to determine that from inside. It might have been her imagination. If Michael had moved her to save her, he might have taken her away from Vegas. She trusted his judgement, even though she shouldn't have. If she could get to the large window, maybe she would recognize the local scenery. The famous Las Vegas Strip that she'd spent so much time galavanting on over the course of the past week would be immediately recognizable.

Instead of dragging herself out of bed and to the window, Amelia suddenly decided she wanted to talk to her mom. Like a scared little girl, she needed to hear her mom's voice speaking words of comfort and encouragement. It felt like an urgent need, one that superseded everything else. Amelia turned to the bedside table nearby to look for a phone. She doubted that her own mobile phone would be there. She figured it had been lost or taken. She was right. But she thought maybe there would be a landline phone. If so, Amelia could call her mom. She knew her mom's number by heart. It was the same number that had been assigned to Diane Baker when she moved to Rosemary Run more than a decade earlier.

Diane and Amelia loved each other as much as any mother and daughter, but their relationship was distant. They didn't talk very often unless one of them needed something from the other. Their connection was based more on the role they played in each other's lives than anything else. Diane called Amelia when she needed help with her alarm system or had a question about one of her bills. Amelia called Diane when she needed scrubs mended or wanted a copy of a family recipe. Many times, Amelia had wished things could be different with her mom. There had been happy childhood days in the past when Diane was Amelia's whole world. Neither of them realistically thought they could get that level of warmth back. Yet, in the deepest corners of their minds, they hoped that somehow they might find a way. Somehow.

Someday. Their relationship wasn't beyond repair. And right now, Amelia needed her mom something fierce.

Gritting her teeth and pushing through the pain, Amelia heaved herself upward to get a full view of the side table. To her relief, a long, thin telephone sat at the ready. She picked it up, careful not to jostle her aching body any more than necessary. Large, smooth buttons sat nestled underneath the receiver. Slowly and deliberately, Amelia dialed Diane's mobile phone number. She knew it by heart. But something was wrong. The call didn't go through. A dead, heavy silence filled the space, then a fast beeping.

"Hello?" Amelia asked against the beeping, more optimistically than she should have. "I want to talk to my mom, Diane Baker. In Rosemary Run, California. Operator? Can you connect me?"

Part of Amelia knew that no one was on the other end of the line. Another part of her was still groggy and confused. All she knew for sure was that her life was a mess. She feared it was beyond repair. And compared to a few short years ago, beyond recognition. Her one hope was that falling in love with Michael could turn things around. He could make things right. He was what she thought she needed more than anything else. She wanted to tell her mom about him. To announce that her life had taken a turn for the good.

Amelia wracked her brain as she tried to figure out what was wrong with the telephone. Maybe she needed to dial a "1" for an outside line. If so, that must mean she was in a hotel. Right? A private residence like a condo shouldn't have an operator or need a private line.

Although, maybe the problem was the long distance, which reminded Amelia that an area code would be necessary. Had she dialed ten digits? Or seven? Frustrated, she dropped the phone onto the side table. The beeping continued.

"Damn this headache and these sore muscles!" she shouted. "I've really got to stop drinking so much. I'm getting too old to party like I used to."

The only good news was that Amelia's wrist injury barely hurt anymore. Maybe it hadn't been as bad as she'd originally thought.

Amelia's outlook oscillated from hopeful to hopeless. She believed she was entirely responsible for her own pain and suffering. It's the only explanation that made any real sense. She was partially right, but there was much more to the story. Turning quickly, she picked up the phone again. She clicked the button on the receiver once. The beeping finally stopped.

"Thank God," she mumbled under her breath.

Gathering her wits, she pressed 0 and waited. If this place was a hotel, some sort of operator or front desk clerk should answer. She counted the seconds the same way she always did when checking a patient's pulse.

One-Mississippi, two-Mississippi, three-Mississippi, four…

"Front desk," a perky female voice on the other end of the line chirped. "How can I help, Mrs. Bell?"

Amelia shook her head, as if she could shake off the various assaults to her senses. The sounds were too loud, the operator's voice too shrill. The lights were too bright, seeming as if they threatened to blind her. But the biggest jolt came from hearing herself called Mrs. Bell.

Amelia's insides suddenly felt gooey and loose, a topsy turvy mix.

"Oh, um, I'm not…"

"What?" the operator asked. "I'm having trouble hearing you. Will you speak up?"

Amelia rolled her eyes and pressed her chin against the phone. "I'm not Mrs. Bell," she said clearly. "I wish."

She heard the sound of papers rustling on the other end of the line, then the clinking of rapid typing.

"I've got it right here in my records," the perky operator said. "Michael Bell stopped by the front desk on his way out and gave instructions for us to get his wife anything she needed."

Amelia's mouth dropped open, she was so shocked.

What in the hell? What's happening?

The news quickly sobered her up. Sure, she had been immediately infatuated with Michael when she met him, but this was getting to be too much. Clearing her throat, Amelia collected herself and affirmed her resolve. She wanted to talk to her mom.

"I want to make a phone call," she said in a strong voice. "I'm having trouble getting an outside line."

"Oh, sure thing," the operator said. "Hang up, then dial a 9 followed by the area code and number. You'll be connected in a jiffy."

"A jiffy?" Amelia asked, chuckling.

She hadn't meant to say it out loud, but the silliness of the word had caught her off guard. She began to think she was still sleeping, and that this was somehow a strange dream.

Actually, that made a lot of sense. Amelia wished she

were dreaming. She wanted to be with Michael, but she didn't want to be groggy and sore. She didn't want to be in a strange bed in a strange hotel or condo or whatever this place was.

She closed her eyes and tried to focus. She'd had dreams before that made her think they were really happening, yet fell away when she finally woke up. They'd seemed completely real when she was in the middle of them. So real that she had honestly thought she was awake and starting her day. Maybe that's what was happening now. Maybe she had such a huge crush on Michael that she wanted to wake up as his wife. Dreaming that would make some sense. It certainly could have been worse.

Sometimes, Amelia had terrifying dreams that gripped her with fear and wouldn't let her escape. She was glad that this dream-- if it was, in fact, a dream-- wasn't one of the frightening sorts. Dens of snakes, rats, and spiders made frequent appearances during Amelia's nighttime hours, along with the sensations of falling from terrifying heights and being stuck in small spaces. It was enough to drive a person crazy, if she'd let it. She'd been dreaming about these things since she was a child.

Diane used to get up with her daughter after a bad dream and then sit dutifully by her bed until Amelia fell back asleep. Amelia had wondered if the bad dreams served to connect mother and daughter. Maybe for that reason, Amelia's subconscious mind had produced more of them. As long as the bad dreams kept coming, there'd be reason for Diane and Amelia to sit together in the wee hours of the night, free from the obligations and busy schedules of daytime. Come to think of it, perhaps that's part of the reason Amelia became a pediatric nurse. During her long shifts at the hospital, she'd spent many a night comforting scared kids as they sat together, moonlight glowing softly outside.

As a nurse, Amelia had often wondered if the darker dreams she'd experienced were actually night terrors. Some people were more prone to them than others, although the medical community doesn't seem to know why. She'd meant to see a sleep specialist to try and get to the bottom of it. They'd ask her to spend the night in a lab, hooked up to wires and monitors. A sleep study would be the only way to find out more about the physiology of what was happening. But like many other things in her life, Amelia had put it off. Putting things off had become her new normal. But that didn't matter now. The task at hand was to focus so she could figure out what was happening.

"You know," the operator said, interrupting Amelia's train of thought, "a jiffy, like really quick. I mean that your call will be connected really quick."

Amelia shook her head. Amelia shook her head. She hadn't needed it spelled out.

"Okay," she replied. "Thank you, ma'am. I'll try that."

"You betcha!" the operator chirped.

The woman was too chipper for her own good, but Amelia figured it worked reasonably well for a front desk clerk. Determined to either wake up or call her mother if she were already awake, Amelia turned back toward the side table. She was about to push the button to hang up the phone when the operator spoke again.

"Oh, good news, Mrs. Bell," the woman said. "Your husband just walked through the door. I'm sure he'll be up in a jiff… I mean, he'll be up to join you soon."

7

Present Day
Rosemary Run, California

"Um, hello," Amelia said sheepishly as she stared up at her husband.

Michael snarled as he towered over the table, Amelia huddled underneath. The scene looked like something out of a James Bond movie-- a villain having tracked down an innocent woman who simply found herself in the wrong place at the wrong time. Truth be told, that could describe Amelia's marriage just as well as the current scene. But this wasn't a movie. It was Amelia's real life. Her terror was real, as was Rebecca's concern for her friend.

"You don't have to go anywhere with him," Rebecca said, standing and positioning herself between Amelia and Michael. "Not if you don't want to."

Michael let a sinister laugh escape his lips. He threw his head back as he laughed, like a jackal. It was obvious to everyone present that he thought he held all the power. He wasn't impressed with Rebecca's attempts to intervene. Michael believed that his wife belonged to him alone. He considered her property. Property he had made an investment in. He intended to see that investment returned.

"Oh, yes she does," Michael said with a roar.

"No, she doesn't," Rebecca replied. "I'm not scared of you, you big oaf. Not one bit."

Amelia shook like a leaf under the table, her wedding ring clanking nervously against one of the metal bars. Rebecca didn't back down. She stood up straight and looked him dead in the eye.

Michael lowered his brow and scanned the room, apparently considering his options. A decent-sized crowd remained in the restaurant. Plenty of people to witness and report on his behavior. He didn't much care about the Rosemary Run Police Department, though. He'd gone toe to toe with police from much larger cities and won. He didn't expect any real or lasting problems from these small town cops. What he didn't want was anyone trying to physically stop him from taking Amelia away. He had plans for her. It was time to leave for the backcountry. He had tried to make the trip sound appealing so she would go willingly. If that wouldn't work, he'd move to plan B.

He turned and squared his body against Rebecca's.

"I suggest you stay out of my business," he said curtly, his voice a growl.

"My friend is my business," Rebecca said. "She doesn't want to go anywhere with you."

Michael slammed a fist down on the table suddenly,

sending silverware crashing to the floor and causing Amelia to jump so much that she hit her head.

"Ouch!" Amelia cried as she raised a hand to the top of her head. "I think I hit a screw or something. That hurt."

Michael smiled and leaned his weight back on his heels like a predator closing in on prey. He seemed to enjoy the fact that Amelia was hurt. He seemed to consider it a successful move on his part. In the game that was manipulating and controlling his wife, a bump on the head served to let her-- and everyone watching-- know that he was calling the shots. That his physical dominance was real and undisputed.

Rebecca glanced around, her eyes searching for James. Her husband should have been there already. What was taking him so long? Michael noticed Rebecca's search. It buoyed him further.

"Who are looking for?" he asked. "Someone to save you? What? Is all that tough talk just an act?"

Rebecca's face flushed. She never should have taken her eyes off Michael's.

"No," she said firmly. "I told you, I'm not afraid of you."

He stepped closer to her, his face inches from hers. She could smell alcohol on his breath.

"Are you drunk?" she asked.

Michael recoiled, disgusted by her nerve. "That's none of your damn business," he shouted.

In her peripheral vision, Rebecca could see an older man a few tables over stand. He appeared to be in his early sixties. He was in good shape-- probably former military or an athlete-- but he was clearly no match for Michael. The man seemed ready to make a move, as if he'd already decided that he had to do something. Rebecca didn't recognize the man and appreciated his willingness to help, but she feared he would get himself hurt if he confronted Michael. Rebecca looked at the man and shook her head. She couldn't let him get tangled up in this mess. It was already bad enough that she and Amelia were ensnared.

Michael's head snapped around to see who Rebecca was eyeing. He let out another sinister laugh as he appraised the man.

"Well, well, well," Michael muttered. "So, we have a wanna-be hero. What are you going to do, old man?" he taunted.

The man lifted his chin high and raised both fists in the air. He seemed determined.

"Leave the ladies alone," he said. "If you want to fight someone, come over here and fight me. I'll give you a lickin' that will teach you a lesson, you prick."

Michael lowered his shoulders and balled his hands into fists. No sooner did he raise one hand in front of him to challenge the old man than another man-- much younger this time-- stood and stepped forward.

"Leave them all alone," the young man said. "Come on, man. You don't really want to do this here. How about you go home and sleep whatever it is off."

Michael sneered once more, apparently seeing himself as invincible. "I'll have you know, I don't appreciate strangers getting in my business," he quipped. "You go home yourself."

The younger man shook his head. He seemed to have just as much confidence in his own ability to handle Michael as Michael did in his ability to control the situation.

"Okay, then," the younger man said, standing alongside the older man and raising his fists in the air. "If it's a fight you want, then you've got it. We aren't going to let you harass these ladies. Not here. Not today."

The old man narrowed his eyes and nodded approvingly at the younger man. They were a team now. Michael was outnumbered. The pair crouched and leaned forward in what looked like respectable fighting positions. A few other guests held up smartphones, ready to record what happened next. This scene was making the evening news, as well as the rounds on social media.

Amelia shuddered under the table. She was mortified by what her quiet lunch with her best friend was turning into. She wanted to get up. To do something to stop all of this. But she was frozen. She knew that the only way to make Michael stop would be to go with him, like he had asked. She had tried to feel good about the backcountry trip with her husband, but she was scared. Michael's temper had escalated to a dangerous level. Amelia couldn't be sure she'd be safe. Not alone. And certainly not isolated in the middle of nowhere. She hadn't wanted anyone to know the severity of her situation, but she feared for her life.

"Michael!" Amelia shouted in the strongest voice she could muster. She hoped she could somehow reason with him. Maybe her voice would cut through and cause him to pay attention. "Please. Don't do this. For me?"

Michael laughed again. It had been too many laughs. He sounded maniacal, and he was making everyone very uncomfortable.

Without saying another word, Michael turned his attention back to Amelia. In one swift motion he reached down, his arm muscles bulging as he lifted the table top with both hands. Using all his might, he threw the table into the air. It flipped, then crashed down hard beside Amelia, narrowly missing her. Six inches to the left, and it would have struck her. Glasses and plates shattered and more silverware clanked against the floor. Amelia cowered, curling into a fetal position with her hands above her head. Shards of glass littered her long brown hair. She gasped for air, the panic overtaking her.

"How dare you cross me?" Michael's voice boomed. "You ought to know better by now, but I guess it's time to teach you a lesson you won't forget."

"No!" Rebecca shouted.

"Don't!" Amelia begged. "Please!"

The good samaritans hovered nearby, calculating their next move.

"Get up! Now!" Michael yelled, at the top of his lungs. "I mean it, Amelia. Get. Up."

Using one strong hand, he reached down and plucked his wife from the debris. She was no match for his physical strength. Once off the floor, he held her by the hair and the upper arm. Amelia writhed in pain as wads of her hair were torn out mercilessly. Michael's handling was rough. He didn't care if Amelia was hurt. In fact, he wanted her to hurt. He wanted her to think twice before disobeying him again.

"Stop this!" Rebecca shouted. "James will find you. You'll be arrested. It will be worse for you if you take her off this property!"

It was no use. Michael ignored Rebecca's pleas. He made his way down to the lower level and towards the front door, dragging Amelia along with him, crying and screaming.

The good samaritan guys looked at each other, unsure of how to handle the situation. It seemed like everyone present had thought Michael could be somehow talked down. No one was prepared for the situation to escalate this far. The younger guy motioned to the older one, then they sprang into action, quickly making their way towards the front door.

"We can't let him get away with her!" the older man shouted to the crowd. "We need more help."

Soon, a trio of other men fell in line, joining the charge. They were five strong now. Enough to pose a serious challenge to Michael's tirade. Michael was incredibly strong, but he was no match for five grown men. At least, so the other men thought. They moved hurriedly, with determination. They were prepared to give it their all. For that, Amelia and Rebecca were grateful.

Rebecca cursed her husband, hoping that James would enter the premises any minute with his gun drawn and reinforcements on the way. She needed him now. Amelia needed him. Hell, everyone in the restaurant needed him. They needed police presence on the scene. What was taking so long?

Rebecca pulled out her phone and fumbled a text:

Where are you? Need RRPD here right away. Michael is dangerous. Taking Amelia against her will.

The message sent with the same familiar swooshing sound as it had earlier. Only the ruckus in the room made it too loud for the effect to be heard. Like she had at her house before she and Amelia left for lunch that day, Rebecca said a silent prayer for her friend. She could only hope that this ended with Amelia safe and Michael behind bars. If only Amelia had listened to Rebecca from the very beginning, none of this would have happened. Rebecca didn't try to chase after Michael. The five men who had taken up the task were better equipped to handle it. She had stalled Michael. She hoped it would be enough.

As the dining room of Marcheline's restaurant devolved into chaos, she looked on from the kitchen. She had called 9-1-1 when Michael first got loud with the hostess. She'd also called her husband, Julien. But Marcheline had a history of her own with violent men who sought to take advantage of vulnerable women. As a teenager, she had fled her home in Illinois after a neighbor and close family friend had molested and threatened her. Running from him had cost decades of time spent without her beloved parents. Not to mention, decades living with the terror of being found by that monster. Marcheline knew her own strength now, and she wouldn't let a guest be harmed, if she could help it. Not at her restaurant. Not on her watch.

Marcheline walked calmly to her office and took the gun that her friend Rande had given her out of the safe. Checking to be certain it was still loaded the way she had left it, she cocked the weapon and placed it in the waistband of her pants at the small of her back. If police weren't here by the time she made her way outside, she intended to use the gun to stop Michael herself. Marcheline didn't think about the risk. In the back of her mind, she knew that Michael might have a weapon also. But this was too important. There was no telling what Michael would do to Amelia if he took her away. Marcheline wouldn't let it happen. She hoped someone would do the same for her daughter or granddaughters if the tables were turned.

As Marcheline hurried out the front door, she noticed that the commotion had only intensified as Michael reached the parking lot. Rebecca stood in the doorway, looking on in horror.

The sight was a heartbreaking one. Amelia sobbed heavily as Michael slung her around by the hair. He pulled her from side to side in front of him, ripping and tearing at her hair without regard for how painful it was. The group of men stood at the ready to attack, but Michael was using his wife as a shield. He slowly backed up towards a black Cadillac SUV, presumably his. The older man who had stood up to Michael first eyed an approach from the side, but his opportunity was thwarted the moment Michael caught on. No police yet. Time was running out.

Marcheline pushed past Rebecca.

"Enough!" she said loudly, her French accent distinctive.

People stopped and took notice. Enough of them recognized her as the owner of the restaurant and winery. Maison du Vin was one of the most popular places in town. Marcheline and Julien had built an honorable reputation for themselves.

"It's the owner!" someone yelled.

"That's right," Marcheline said, stepping out into the open and raising the gun in front of her. "And it's time for this little disturbance to end, my darlings."

8

A Year Prior, Back Then
Las Vegas, Nevada

Michael's face glistened in the sun as he sat on the side of Amelia's bed. Sheer curtains softened the light as it entered the room, highlighting Michael's handsome features in an ethereal way. Amelia thought he looked good enough to be photographed. If only a professional photographer had been there to capture him in this light.

Michael had the good looks to be featured in any magazine, on any billboard, or in any television show or film. As she stared up at this magnificent physical specimen of a man, Amelia affirmed the assessment she had made the moment she first laid eyes on him. Michael Bell was the most handsome man she'd ever seen. Except for maybe Troy. But she didn't want to think about her ex right now.

"Michael, you're here," she said, rubbing her bleary eyes.

She'd been awake for a while now-- if this was waking life and not a dream-- but she still felt groggy. It was a grogginess she hadn't quite felt before. It was like a hangover, yet different. Amelia knew she'd been drinking heavily the night before. That much, she could remember. Other details were still fuzzy.

"Of course, I am, dear," Michael replied, reaching forward and brushing a few errant strands of brown hair out of Amelia's eyes. "Where else would I be?"

He leaned down and kissed her gently on the lips. His touch sent a wave of pleasure through her being. She was confused though. It didn't feel like the first time. She would have wanted to savor their first kiss. Surely, it hadn't passed her by without being remembered.

Amelia smiled.

"Are you hungry?" Michael asked.

She nodded. She wasn't sure she actually was hungry, but she wanted to please him.

The front desk clerk's use of the name Mrs. Bell nagged at Amelia. She had a million questions she wanted to ask Michael, but she didn't want to be a bother. She hardly knew him and didn't want to overwhelm him. Other men had told her she was too much. Too needy. Too high maintenance. She had vowed to take better care to hide her own desires. Maybe that's what had spilled over into other aspects of her life. If she put other people before herself, Amelia thought maybe bad things wouldn't happen to her. Maybe she'd be spared the gut-wrenching emotional pain like what she and Troy had gone through.

Like what she'd experienced as a child. But she didn't want to think about any of that right now either.

Amelia's thoughts turned to the night she'd spent making love to the female showgirl. That woman-- Val was her name-- had understood Amelia in a way that no man could. Amelia could feel the camaraderie. The being in-sync. She had been incredibly turned on by the showgirl and she had enjoyed their connection immensely. In fact, she wondered why she'd waited so long to take a sexy woman to bed. She got the idea that a lesbian relationship would afford some hefty advantages when it came to mutual respect and understanding, but for better or worse, Amelia preferred men. Especially when it came to long-term relationships and marriage, Amelia wanted a man. A rugged, confident man.

"I'll call down and have room service send something," Michael said. "Bacon and eggs? Maybe some toast? And juice."

Amelia didn't eat much meat. She wasn't a full-blown vegetarian, but she preferred something lighter. Maybe oatmeal and fruit with yogurt and a large glass of ice water. Bacon and eggs sounded too heavy for her battered stomach. Whatever had happened last night clearly did a number on her body.

"I think I'd like oatmeal instead, if you don't mind," she said in a timid voice. She was afraid to upset Michael.

He laughed. She barely knew him yet. She wasn't sure what to make of it.

"Nonsense," he replied. "You're getting bacon and eggs."

He picked up the phone and placed the order.

Amelia sat stunned. He had just overruled her breakfast order. She found it odd, and somewhat insulting. She quickly considered bringing it up and challenging him, but thought better of it. She kept her mouth shut and moved on. Her thoughts immediately turned to the fact that she'd thought it was mid-day based on the sun's location in the sky. Why was Michael ordering breakfast this late? Was he being extra considerate albeit in a pushy way, or was she in some kind of strange time warp?

"Now," Michael said once breakfast was on the way. "Why don't you get dressed, and we'll get this honeymoon started?"

Amelia froze, stunned. How could this be? She oscillated back to the possibility of this being one strange dream. How could it be waking life? What on Earth could have happened to make her Michael's wife when she had zero memory of it? Where was Rebecca? For that matter, where was Amelia right now? And why did she feel like she'd been run over by a truck?

"Um, what do you mean?" she asked Michael cautiously.

Amelia was aware of the potential to upset Michael. He struck her as a person who was accustomed to getting exactly what he wanted. She doubted he ever wanted for anything. He probably had women lined up around the block to take her place should she ever fail to appreciate her good fortune in having the privilege to be with him.

"About getting dressed?" he asked, then chuckled and kissed her on the end of her nose. "You don't want to go out in that, do you? I mean, I might like it, but I'd probably get jealous when all the men drool over you. I don't think my ego could take it."

Wasn't that the truth?

Amelia looked down at her body for the first time since she'd woken up. She was dressed in a low cut satin nightgown. It did little to hide the bruises. She tensed, suddenly aware of the physical evidence that matched her level of pain. Michael stared at her pensively, his face taut and his intensity boring into her. She laughed nervously, unsure how to respond.

"I meant about the honeymoon?" she asked, gathering her courage. "You don't mean a real honeymoon, do you? I mean… we aren't actually *married*, are we? Because I don't remember…"

His face relaxed again, and it reminded her of an actor playing a part. Michael was handsome enough to be an actor. Amelia hoped he wasn't actually faking the sincerity during their interactions. She hoped he actually liked her and wasn't just pretending. If his feelings weren't genuine, what would he want with her, anyway?

He raised a finger and pressed it to her lips.

"Shh," he said. "Too many questions. Get dressed in something pretty. Breakfast will be here by the time you get out of the shower. And your questions will be answered soon enough."

"I… I don't have my suitcase here…" Amelia continued. "It was in my hotel room with Rebecca. I was packing to return home to Rosemary Run. I'm not sure…"

She suddenly wondered if she should be telling him where she was from. Too late now.

"Not to worry," he said. "I had some clothes brought. You'll find them in the wardrobe by the window. You're a size eight, right?"

How did he know? And where in the world did he find the clothes? Amelia was unsure whether he meant her clothes from her suitcase, or new clothes that he purchased for her. Either way, it seemed strange. Again, she decided not to upset him.

"Yes. Thank you," she said. I just…"

"What?"

Amelia took a big breath, summoning all the courage she could. She was afraid that she might say something that would set him off. But there were certain things she had to know.

"Are we still in Las Vegas?" she asked.

Michael sighed, a look of irritation overtaking his face. "Amelia, my dear," he replied. "Stop worrying so much. Live a little. Let go and find the flow. Let's enjoy this beautiful day."

Amelia wanted to scream, but she held it in. She remembered the way the bar patrons had responded when Michael walked through the door. This man was well known and liked by many people. She should probably trust him. Besides, she had wanted to be with him. She was getting her wish. She told herself to calm down and go with the flow, as Michael had suggested. She forced a smile, thinking of that phone call to her mom and hoping she wasn't making a big mistake.

"Okay, fine," she said in the most enthusiastic tone she could manage. "What do you have planned?"

He shook his head no and wagged a finger in the air at her. "No more questions."

"Right," she confirmed. "Got it."

Michael smiled, then left the room to give her privacy. The move struck Amelia as odd. If they were really married, and that hadn't been their first kiss, why would he leave the room while she showered and dressed? Wouldn't a new husband be all over his wife? Wouldn't a newlywed couple want to shower together, making passionate love before heading out for the day? At least, that's how Amelia had imagined it when she'd been engaged to Troy. And there he was, forcing himself into her thoughts despite her best efforts to purge him from her memory.

Not even Rebecca knew what had happened with Troy. Amelia's friend probably thought she knew, but she didn't. Amelia had kept that tragedy under lock and key. For good reason. It had been the most devastating experience of Amelia's entire life. In fact, her breakup wasn't because she didn't want to be with Troy anymore. Quite the contrary.

Amelia had broken up with Troy because it was too painful to look at him after the loss they'd suffered. She couldn't begin to imagine how they'd ever be whole and healed again, so she ran away. She'd told Rebecca parts of the story-- true parts-- but she hadn't shared the magnitude of the heartbreak. It's what had sent Amelia into the string of lackluster boyfriends and meaningless dates in the first place. Troy had been real. But nothing since had been anything more than sex and physical attraction. Until Michael and whatever this was. Amelia hoped that her connection with Michael was real. She desperately wanted it to be.

Aches and pains seized Amelia as she tried to turn over in the bed. She wasn't sure how she'd make it through a shower. She glanced at the phone again, considering whether she had time to try her mom. Telling someone where she was made sense. It was a prudent, good idea. She picked up the phone, the dial tone sounding loudly from the receiver. Amelia got as far as remembering to dial 9 for an outside line and then entering the first four digits of her mom's number before she stopped herself and set the phone down. She couldn't call her mom when she didn't even know where she was or what had happened to her. What would she tell Diane, exactly? That she was with a man she really liked and thought might be the one, yet she couldn't remember the night before and had no idea where she was or how she got there? That would sound insane. Not to mention, the bruises and the talk of being Mrs. Bell on a honeymoon. Amelia made the decision for certain. She'd figure out what was going on before she contacted her mom. Or Rebecca.

With that out of the way, Amelia turned her attention back to getting out of the bed and into the shower. It was going to be difficult. Pain caught her as she rolled to the edge of the bed. The more awake she became, the more she could feel specific pain in specific places. Her ribs hurt, as if she'd been kicked hard. Her lower back hurt, too, as if she'd been hit right in a kidney. And her throat was sore.

Oh, yeah, Amelia thought, suddenly remembering the

large man who had grabbed her up by the throat just before she'd blacked out. She couldn't place the other injuries, but that one had a memory attached. Was it real, though? Had that really happened? Had Michael saved her from an assault, and if so, why was he being so cagey about it? Shouldn't he be glad that she was okay? Why wouldn't he let her ask questions?

She had so many questions. Far more questions than answers.

9

Something remarkable happens to people in crisis situations when the trauma is too much to process or comprehend. They begin to detach from themselves, emotionally distancing to preserve whatever sense of safety they can. Survivors who have experienced it talk in terms of leaving their bodies or going away someplace else in their minds. It's a protective mechanism for our psyches. Ultimately, it's a good thing. But no one wants trauma at that level. Not if they can help it. In extreme cases, the personality can become permanently fractured.

Amelia had seen it happen. As a pediatric nurse, she'd treated children who had been beaten, run over by cars, mauled by wild animals, and all manner of other horrors that no child should have to go through. She knew the mind's protective distancing could happen in adults, too, although she hadn't seen that first hand. Until that day at Maison du Vin as Michael slung her around by the hair in front of a gasping crowd. It was then that Amelia, too, found herself going far away in her mind. It was the only escape she could make.

Michael had Amelia in his grips, the pain from her torn hair and jostled neck too much to bear. And the fear... It was overwhelming. Amelia's fight or flight response had kicked in the moment she'd heard Michael's voice booming throughout the restaurant. Only fighting wasn't an option for her. She thought Michael was too strong. Too powerful. He certainly was both. Some other women of Amelia's size would have chosen a physical fight to give it all they had. She was tall and physically fit. And she could have used her wits and intelligence to fight smarter rather than harder. But Amelia's assessment of the situation was that she didn't have a prayer of successfully fighting the man. In part, this was due to the relentless abuse and manipulation she'd endured during the year they'd been together. Flight, then, was the other option. Except that she was trapped. Just like in her nightmares. How horrible. What cruel fate.

Amelia closed her eyes, drifting off, even though her body was still being tossed around violently. She leaned into the mental escape and felt her essence moving far away. It was a strange feeling. She could still hear the sounds around her, yet they were distant, fading gradually into the background. Like falling asleep. Soon, the scene at Maison du Vin seemed like it was happening to someone else.

Thank God, she thought.

Marcheline now had everyone's attention, thanks to her weapon and commanding presence. Her body language was confident. Her resolve was sure. She obviously knew how to handle a gun. The crowd watched with bated breath, unsure of what to do or what they were about to witness. Several more diners from indoors made their way outside. They slinked along the front wall of the building, curious, but afraid at the same time.

Michael was the one person who should have taken notice of Marcheline's stance. She aimed to stop him and she meant business. Unfortunately, he paid her little attention. Undeterred by Marcheline's threats, Michael continued to pull Amelia towards his truck. He was determined to take his wife away. He squinted against the bright sun, turning away from Marcheline, his eyes focused on the door handle of his vehicle. He was nearly close enough to reach out and touch it. Within seconds, he was there, his hand on the shiny silver handle. If someone didn't act fast, he'd have Amelia in the truck and on her way out of town.

"Where are our police?" Rebecca asked, exasperated, from her position in the doorway.

Rebecca pulled her phone out again and dialed 9-1-1 to ask for an update and communicate the urgency of the situation. Once that was done, she'd try James. Something must have delayed him. It didn't make sense. He should have been here by now. *Someone* should have been here by now. 9-1-1 calls had been placed. Rebecca's head spun as she tried to figure it out. The hairs on the back of her neck stood on end. Something was wrong.

The good samaritan men who had banded together to

help stood motionless as they waited to see what Marcheline was going to do. No one wanted to get in the line of fire, that much was certain. Each of them knew that someone should step forward and take the lead, but the personal risk in doing so was climbing higher by the minute. Not to mention, it was hard for them to know exactly what to do. They judged that Matcheline had the gun and thus the best chance to put an end to the drama.

"Screw you!" Michael yelled in Marcheline's direction. "I'm leaving this place, and I'm taking my wife with me. There isn't a damn thing you can do about that. She's mine. She wants to be with me. She chose me. She married me."

"No, you're not going anywhere," Marcheline said. "Let the lady go."

Marcheline held the gun out in front of her, lowered her brows, and took aim. She intended to shoot out Michael's tires, but she was still too far away. There were too many people in between who could get hurt. Marcheline wanted to see Amelia saved, but she wouldn't act hastily and injure innocent people in the process. Doing so would make things worse, not better.

"Damn," Marcheline said under her breath, glancing at Rebecca. "They're too far. Did you call the authorities?"

"Yes!" Rebecca shouted, the frustration evident in her voice. "I don't know what's keeping them."

Marcheline pursed her lips and steeled herself. "Then I must go," she mumbled.

Rebecca looked at her intently. The two women shared a moment of understanding between them. Their eyes communicated volumes. They were both dedicated to saving Amelia. Rebecca wanted to help because Amelia was her best friend. Marcheline was set on helping because she'd vowed to never cower from an abusive man again. Plus, Marcheline took it as a personal insult that Michael would come into Maison du Vin and disrespect her place of business and her patrons like he had.

"I'll go with you," Rebecca said.

It was a snap judgment on her part. She didn't have kids of her own to think about. She wanted them, sure. But no one's life would be permanently damaged if she should be seriously injured or killed that day. James would grieve. He'd be devastated, but he'd move on. His sister Cate and her family would help him with that. Someone needed to stand up for Amelia. She was in over her head. Rebecca knew she was no physical match for Michael, but teamed up with Marcheline and her weapon, the two of them might just stand a chance.

Marcheline considered Rebecca for a minute. She looked her up and down, assessing her physical strength and presence.

"She's your friend?" Marcheline asked.

"My best friend," Rebecca replied. "She's like a sister to me. I'd do anything for her."

Marcheline hesitated another few seconds, playing out possible scenarios in her mind.

"Do you know how to use a gun?" Marcheline asked.

"Honestly, not really," Rebecca said. "My husband is a cop and I know what he's told me about guns, but I've shied away from them myself. But don't let that concern you. I'm scrappy. I'll figure out a way to help you. I could create a distraction…"

This pleased Marcheline. She nodded.

"Okay, let's move."

Rebecca nodded back, then fell in step behind Marcheline as the pair made their way into the parking lot and toward Michael's truck. People stepped out of their path when they saw them coming. By the looks on their faces, the crowd was relieved to see someone taking action. Several of them followed Marcheline and Rebecca as if they might jump in to assist should they identify an opportunity to make a difference.

As they neared Michael's truck, the good samaritan men took notice. They, too, seemed relieved.

"Ms. Fay," one of the men began, "what's your plan, ma'am?"

"How can we help?" asked another.

"We're at your service ma'am," said a third. "We just want to help the lady."

Marcheline nodded at the men, so much being communicated without words.

"Follow me," she said as she quickly walked the final distance to the area where Michael's truck was parked.

Time was running out. Michael had unlocked and opened the driver's side door and was in the process of hoisting Amelia inside. Marcheline and Rebecca could see Amelia's face now. Her eyes had glazed over, opening and closing lethargically. It looked like she might have suffered a head injury. She didn't look good at all. Rebecca again wondered where the authorities were.

"She needs medical attention!" Rebecca shouted, loud enough for Michael to hear.

"Yes, she sure does," Marcheline confirmed, raising her voice as she continued her approach. She lowered her weapon slightly, hoping she might appeal to whatever shred of decency remained in Amelia's attacker. "Michael? That's your name, right?"

He turned slightly, grunting. He didn't slow down more than a tiny bit. Michael knew he needed to keep moving and get out of there for his plan to be a success. He didn't answer Marcheline. Instead, he picked Amelia up by the arms and pushed her into the truck. Her long brown hair and long limbs dangled out. She didn't resist as he tried to stuff the parts of her into the cab.

"That's right," Rebecca confirmed. "His name is Michael. Michael Bell." Catching on to Marcheline's tactics, Rebecca offered what she knew. "He loves her. I know that much. I've seen that love in his eyes. I was there when they got married. It was a beautiful ceremony. It took place outdoors under hundred-year-old oaks."

Marcheline raised one eyebrow, then quickly washed her expression back to a neutral one. Was Rebecca serious? Serious or not, she might be onto something.

"I imagine he cares for her very much. He married her," Marcheline added, her voice quieter now. "You love her, don't you, Michael?"

Marcheline and Rebecca were working hard to deescalate the situation. They only had mere minutes to do so before violence became the only option. The group of guys looked at Marcheline, waiting for her cue. They trusted in her leadership and were visibly relieved that someone had taken charge. They stood at the ready.

"Shut your mouth," Michael snarled. "You don't know nothing."

Marcheline's eyebrow reacted again, apparently unable to help itself. She got it under control quickly, returning to a neutral expression once more. Rebecca eyed Marcheline, hoping to impress upon her the seriousness of the threat.

"She's only saying out loud what we all see," Rebecca said. "It's obvious that you care very much. You didn't mean to hurt Amelia. You're just frustrated right now. We get that."

The ladies held their breath, wondering what Michael would do next. He narrowed his eyes as he considered what they were saying. But he didn't stop moving. He pushed Amelia over to the passenger seat, her head drooping down onto her chest. Her body posture was unnatural, and alarming.

"We…" Marcheline began again, talking more rapidly now. "We think she may be hurt. That she might need to see a doctor. You want that for your wife, right, Michael?"

"Don't call me that," he replied angrily. "You don't know me. You don't even know my wife. Stay out of our business."

He climbed into the truck, then closed the door hard behind him.

"Michael," Rebecca pleaded. "Let us take her to the hospital. Please."

He shook his head.

"I mean it!" Rebecca continued. "Once she's all better,

the two of you can travel the backcountry, just like you wanted."

Michael ignored Rebecca's pleas, digging keys out of his pocket and then starting the ignition. He placed one hand on the steering wheel and looked ahead, ready to pull out of the parking lot and drive away. He didn't seem to be hearing what Marcheline and Rebecca were saying. He was focused on getting Amelia and getting out of there.

"What do we do?" the older man asked. "We can't let him take her away!"

Rebecca considered throwing herself on the hood of Michael's truck, but she hesitated. He just might run her over without a second thought. She wasn't ready to give up on her friend though. Thinking quickly, she eyed the bed of the truck.

Marcheline was thinking quickly, too. She raised her weapon again, debating what to do with it. She had always believed that you shouldn't pull a weapon as a threat if you weren't prepared to use it. Her friend Rande had taught her that. He had lived in Wyoming and knew how to shoot with the best of them. She had fully intended to shoot Michael and his tires if necessary. But now that the moment was here and all of these innocent bystanders were huddled around, she hesitated. Her actions in this moment could affect the lives of numerous people. There was Amelia to think about, of course, but police could pursue and recover her. What if a bullet ricocheted and hit someone in the crowd? They could be fatally injured. Even an attempt to shoot out a tire could end in tragedy. Amelia was injured, for sure, but her life wasn't in immediate danger. At least, Marcheline hoped not. Not yet.

"I'm considering my options," Marcheline said to the others. "It's too dangerous to take a shot."

The older man shook his head, exasperated. He was thinking the same thing as Rebecca. He was ready to take action.

"Get the license plate number!" someone shouted from a distance.

Marcheline lowered her gun, defeated. "I can't take the shot. I wish I could. It wouldn't be a wise decision. I'm sorry, my darlings."

Rebecca and the older man shot each other a look that said it was go time. Moving swiftly, they ran around to the back of the truck. The older man helped Rebecca into the bed, then climbed in after her. They crouched in the back and braced for the ride as Michael hit the accelerator and sped away.

10

———

A Year Prior, Back Then
Las Vegas, Nevada

Showering was a chore. Amelia was so sore and weak. She had to muster every bit of her energy reserves to get through it. She knew she must, though. She didn't want to disappoint Michael. She also didn't want to anger him.

As she toweled off in front of the large mirror in the bathroom, she caught a full view of her bruises for the first time. She was covered in them from head to toe.

My God, she thought. *What happened to me?*

The harshness of her reflection made Amelia weak in the knees. She'd seen bruising like this in the hospital. She never thought she would see it in the mirror. This was beyond anything in her nightmares. Tears springing to her eyes, she flopped onto the floor and hugged her knees against her chest. Pain seared with every movement. She looked around the room, her eyes searching like a frightened animal. Amelia didn't know what she was searching for, but she knew she was in too deep. The reality sat on her like a lead weight. She needed help.

Certain now that this wasn't just a bad dream she was stuck in, Amelia renewed her resolve to contact her mom. If she couldn't do it from the room, she'd find a way during her outing with Michael. She'd tell Diane about the strange happenings in the hopes that she'd know what to do. And if Diane didn't, maybe she'd get in touch with Rebecca. Amelia wanted desperately to hear a friendly voice right now. Even better, she'd love to see a friendly face.

"Dear," Michael called sweetly, rapping on the outside of the bathroom door. "Are you almost ready? I don't want the day to get away from us."

Amelia gasped, tears running down her face. She knew she'd need to get herself together. She couldn't let Michael see her like this. She still wasn't sure if he was the man of her dreams, or something more sinister. Red flags and alarm bells were everywhere, but Amelia wanted so badly to believe that she and Michael had a bright future.

"I'm almost done," she replied, wiping her tears. "I'll be ready soon."

"Good enough," he said playfully. "I can't wait to see you wearing the dress I got you. Have you put it on yet?"

Dress? Amelia didn't know he'd bought her a dress. She hoped it covered the bruises. Otherwise, she couldn't possibly wear it out in public.

"Not yet," she said simply. "Go ahead downstairs. I'll find you."

Maybe she'd have a chance to make a phone call if Michael would leave the room again.

"No need," he said. "I'm content to wait on you here… My beautiful bride."

Now he'd actually said it. They were married. *But how? When?* Amelia wracked her brain as she tried to remember. For lack of a better explanation, she decided the ceremony must have taken place in one of the famous Vegas wedding chapels. She must have been too inebriated to remember. Michael remembered though. So, why didn't she? Surely, there would have been some glimmer in her memory of what had happened after the big man grabbed Amelia by the throat and picked her up off the sofa. That was real. At least, she sure thought so. But it was getting harder and harder to tell.

Amelia told herself that she must suck it up. She dried her tears and forced herself to stand. Moving gingerly, she dried her long hair, then put on the clothes she had brought into the bathroom with her. She'd pulled them from a drawer in the bedroom on her way to the shower. Even though she hadn't recognized the items as her own and still didn't know where her suitcase was, she had decided not to ask questions. After all, Michael had let her know in no uncertain terms that he wouldn't entertain questions. She'd have to find another way to learn what she needed to know.

Amelia winced as she pulled linen pants over her sore legs and a short-sleeve silk top over her chest. The clothes fit.

Interesting, she thought.

She assumed the weather outside was warm enough to

go without long sleeves. She still wasn't sure if she was in Las Vegas though. Dark purple bruises covered the exposed skin around her neck and shoulders. She'd need to find a sweater to cover them up. For that reason, it would be better if the weather outside was cold. She could disguise her body's hurts in cold-weather clothing much more easily. A scarf or a turtleneck would be ideal at this point. She definitely wanted more coverage than a dress would likely provide.

Maybe Amelia could talk Michael into letting her wear these clothes instead of the dress. The pants came all the way down to her ankles. With the addition of a sweater, she would feel, at least, partially covered.

"Okay," Amelia called out to Michael. "I have clothes in here. I'll be out soon."

"Okay," he replied.

Gathering courage, Amelia called to him once more. "Say, did you happen to get him a sweater? Or a shawl? Anything like that?"

Michael didn't respond right away. The delay made Amelia nervous.

Suddenly, she heard rustling outside the bathroom door, then fiddling with the lock. Within less than a minute, Michael had the door open and was staring at Amelia. Her stomach sank. He was invading her privacy. And it wasn't lost on her that she had devolved to the point of believing that she needed his permission for things as simple as choosing an outfit for the day. Amelia was an intelligent, educated woman with a respectable career. How had it come to this? How had she let herself get into this situation?

"What are you doing?" she asked.

He scowled, then quickly pasted a fake smile on his face. He was a handsome man. Even though part of her was afraid of him now, Amelia felt a surge of longing as she looked at Michael. He had a charming smile, fake or not. And there was a magnetism she couldn't deny.

"I'm checking on you," he said.

Remembering the bruises, Amelia wrapped her arms around her shoulder in an attempt to cover them. As she did, Michael stepped closer. So close that Amelia could smell his aftershave. It was a sweet, clean scent.

"Oh?" she asked.

It was all she could come up with. She was confused. Conflicted.

Placing his hands gently on Amelia's waist, Michael pulled her hips against his. It surprised her. She startled, but then began to relax into him. This was what she'd wanted, after all. It was what she'd envisioned. She told herself to remain open. This could be it. The beginning of the rest of her life. A happy relationship that would be the envy of her friends and loved ones. A chance to show them that she wasn't irrevocably broken after what happened with Troy. Perhaps most of all, to convince herself.

"You look amazing," Michael said softly, leaning down and resting his plump lips near Amelia's ear.

He was several inches taller than her. Tall enough for Amelia to wear high heels and still be shorter. That was an unusual find for a woman with such a tall stature. Amelia liked it. She found everything about Michael sexy and appealing.

"That's nice of you to say," she replied.

She wasn't feeling as confident as she usually would have with a man she was attracted to. During her week in Vegas when she'd flirted with, seduced, and bedded numerous strangers, she'd been self assured. Never for a minute had she hesitated when it was time to do the back and forth dance that led to their mutual physical pleasure. But she wasn't self assured now. Not here. There was too much more to this story. Too much that she didn't begin to understand. She was a bundle of nerves. She knew what was coming, but she wasn't sure it was best. She wasn't sure how to handle it.

"I know something else that would be nice," Michael said as he moved his hands around to her backside and gave it a slow, seductive squeeze.

Amelia's body seemed like it might short circuit from all of the mixed messages it was sending and receiving. Michael turned her on, that was for sure. In this very moment, her body warmed to his touch as pressure built between her legs. She wanted him. Yet the pain from the bruises was so intense that she couldn't imagine having sex anytime soon. It would likely be too painful. Couldn't he see how badly hurt she was? She told herself that maybe the light had been too dim for him to see the marks on her body, even though she knew that wasn't true. The sun had been shining in the window beside the bed where he saw her just a little while before.

Amelia laughed nervously, pulling back and meeting Michael's gaze. "I'm not sure what you mean," she said, stalling.

He kept his hands firmly in place. She could feel him

growing against her, his bulge large and insistent. Amelia got the feeling that Michael was a man you didn't say no to. If he wanted sex, it was probably wise to accommodate his wishes. She suspected that his appetite was ravenous. She didn't want to miss her chance to connect with him. And she didn't want to anger him by refusing his advances. But she was uncertain about moving forward. If she could just get some perspective and understand more about the new world she found herself in, then maybe she could let down her guard and proceed without hesitation.

"You know what I mean," he said, smiling.

Michael pulled her against him even more tightly, then kissed her deeply on the mouth. Gently, he slid both hands under her silky top and lifted it over her head. She wasn't wearing a bra. Amelia's exposed breasts perked at his touch, but at the same time, the sore places on her torso sent searing pain throughout her body. Again, she wondered how she could have sex in this condition. She had so many mixed emotions.

"Ouch," she mumbled, unable to help herself.

She hoped he'd stop and ask her what was wrong. That he'd acknowledge the bruises... maybe even explain them. He was using a gentle touch, for which she was grateful. But she needed him to care for her even more tenderly. Whatever had happened to her body was significant. She was hurt too badly to go on as if nothing was wrong. Truth be told, she probably needed to see a doctor. The level of pain she was experiencing might have indicated internal injuries.

To Amelia's dismay, Michael didn't respond to her mention of being in pain. He acted like he hadn't even heard her, his hands moving over her body hungrily, gripping and pulling with desire. His manhood seemed to grow ever harder as he pressed her against the vanity and pressed himself against her.

"You're a fine piece of ass," he said. "Do you know that?"

His choice of words both turned Amelia on and sent more alarm bells off in her head. Was this just an incredibly sexy man who liked to talk a little dirty? In general, Amelia would have been down for that. She was a sexual creature. And she didn't mind walking on the wild side. She liked to be desired. She craved it, even. But Michael's tone also reeked of a controlling man who thought he was entitled to do whatever he wanted to women whenever he wanted to do it. Amelia didn't want that kind of relationship. Or did she?

She shifted her weight, pulling back from him then finding she had nowhere to go. Michael intended to have her right then and there. That much was clear. Using both hands, he tugged her linen pants and panties off, leaving her completely naked and exposed. Her aching muscles tensed as he jostled her and more pain traveled through her body. At the same time, she became wet, more aroused and ready for him to enter her.

What was this strange mixture of pain and pleasure? And what should she do about it?

Amelia had never experienced anything like this before. Sex had always been pleasurable *and* comfortable. Like most other women her age, she'd heard of BDSM and she'd read *Fifty Shades of Grey*. She was aware that some people enjoy heightened arousal and sexual satisfaction when it was coupled with pain. Nipple clamps, ball gags, and the like reportedly sold well at adult toy stores. But was that kind of pleasurable pain what she was feeling?

Would this be-- dare she say it-- nonconsensual sex? Or would it be the best sex of her life? It appeared that she was about to find out.

11

Present Day
Rosemary Run, California

As Michael's truck sped out of the Maison du Vin parking lot, his tires squealed, flinging gravel in every direction. He drove as fast as he could in the hopes that no one would move quickly enough to follow.

He'd asked his business associate, Omar Cox, to create a diversion that would occupy local police. Apparently, Omar had been successful. There was no sign of officers from the Rosemary Run Police Department, despite what Michael assumed were several calls for assistance. He'd seen the concern in the eyes of the crowd. He knew they'd had their smartphones in hand, some dialing while others took photos and videos. He didn't much care. He believed himself to be above the law. If the F.B.I. hadn't been able to pin anything on him by now, he didn't believe small town cops would pose a threat. Not really.

Michael glanced over at Amelia. Her eyes were rolled back in her head and she didn't appear to be conscious. *She'll come around*, he thought. He was convinced she would ultimately meet his every need, including his need for a cover story that would allow him to conduct business in Northern California. It had worked for months now. It was time to go off the grid now and to take the next step in securing his pipeline.

To achieve his criminal dreams, Michael needed to become a ghost for a while. A ghost hiding in plain sight. He'd procured a motor home and he intended to travel the backcountry with Amelia while handling his business affairs discreetly. If anyone came sniffing around, he'd tell them he was a nature enthusiast on an extended trip with his lovely wife. No one would be any the wiser, he was certain.

To be sure plenty of people knew about their travel plans and believed them to be innocuous, Michael had made a big deal of asking Amelia to go away with him. He'd told her romantic stories about how they'd hike by day, sit around the campfire at night, and make love under the stars. She'd believed him. She'd even hoped that things between them might take a turn for the better. That somehow, traveling the backcountry would bring them closer together. Michael was largely indifferent to those hopes. He had what he considered to be more important things on his mind.

"You little cunt," Michael snarled at Amelia, even though she wasn't conscious to hear him. "You nearly ruined everything. Now there's doubt about me. They think I'm a bad guy. They'll try and come after me."

The truck labored as it got up to full speed on the open road, practically groaning with the effort. The vehicle wasn't built for speed and Michael was too hard on it, much like he was on everything and everyone else.

"That's okay," he continued, directing his words at Amelia, but really just talking to himself. "I'm not giving up that easily. I've foiled plenty of people who thought they'd get the best of me. I made it through before, and I'll do it again. Just you wait. You'll be by my side to see my plans come to fruition. I'm not letting you go until I'm done with you."

His words were muffled by the cab, so Rebecca and the older man couldn't make out what Michael was saying. They huddled in the bed of the truck, holding on tightly and working hard to formulate a plan.

"I'm Shane," the man offered, extending a hand for Rebecca to shake. "Shane Baxter. Former Marine Corp Major and later owner of a home security company. I'm retired now. Well, mostly. It's hard to retire completely when you own your own business."

"Rebecca Tatum," she replied. "Pleased to meet you, Major Baxter."

"Please, call me Shane," he said. "I think we're on a first name basis given our... circumstances. Don't you?"

Rebecca laughed. "I suppose you're right."

Wind whipped over the bed of the truck making it hard for Shane and Rebecca to hear each other without shouting. They leaned the heads close together, an instant camaraderie developing between them. Luckily, it was a sunny day without any sign of rain. The air was cool, but not cold. All things considered, it was good weather for a couple of stowaways in the back of a pickup truck.

"So, what made a lovely lady like you decide to hop in the back of a pickup truck on this autumn afternoon?"

Rebecca chuckled. She liked Shane. He reminded her of her Uncle Bob, who was a good natured, jovial man. They'd always been close even though Bob lived across the country in Massachusetts. Shane also reminded Rebecca of her father-in-law, Ron Tatum. She felt at ease around him.

"Blame it on my husband being a cop," Rebecca said. "I've seen and heard more than most. That's my best friend in there. I know the statistics about what happens if an abductor takes an abductee to a second location. It never goes well. I couldn't let them get away."

"Then we're on the same page," Shane replied.

"Good," she said. "I just wish my friend and I had stayed in today and ordered Garfield's Pizza like we talked about instead of going out. Things might have been different. You and I could be meeting at the grocery store right now, or some other normal place."

"Agreed," he confirmed. "Do you have a phone? Have you contacted your husband?"

"I do and I have," Rebecca said. "James hasn't replied. Something is strange about the timing. He should have arrived at Maison du Vin by now… with reinforcements. Where were the EMTs, anyway? Fire department? Anything? I know calls were placed."

"I don't have my phone on me," Shane said. "Left it in my car. I'm old school like that. I was with a date and wanted to give him my full attention."

Rebecca raised her brows. "A date, eh? Would I know the lucky gentleman?"

Shane smiled. "I doubt it. He's from Petaluma. We met on a plane, of all places."

"Nice," she replied. "What better place to meet someone? I like it."

Shane nods, readjusting his grip as the truck tumbles down a curvy road. It's a gorgeous day. Colorful leaves whiz by overhead as they travel. It's a shame that Amelia is trapped in such a dangerous situation on such a pretty day. It's also a shame that Rebecca and Shane had to risk themselves to help her. Neither of them regrets having jumped in the back of the truck though. They're both glad they did.

"Let's come up with a game plan so I can get back to my beau and finish lunch," Shane says. "What are you thinking?"

"Well, I suppose I should try again to get some help," Rebecca said. "This phone ought to be our biggest asset. I'll try 9-1-1."

Shane nods his agreement and they wait for the call to connect. Only, it never does.

"What's that about?" Rebecca asks.

"Maybe we're too far out of town already," Shane tries. "I'm born and raised in Rosemary Run, and I know we've always had poor cell service outside of town. The forest is too dense for the mobile phone companies to do much about it."

They both look up at the trees overhead. While beautiful, Shane is exactly right. Those beautiful trees make getting a cell phone signal difficult. If Michael continues to drive east like he is now, there won't be any signal for a long time. Depending on where he stops, only a satellite phone will work.

"I don't suppose you have a satellite phone?" Shane asks, already knowing the answer.

He's a pleasant man. His demeanor is calm, even in the face of what seem like insurmountable obstacles. Rebecca is glad to have him here with her.

"I'm afraid not," she replies. "I guess we won't be able to contact anyone. And I admit, I didn't think that part through. What are we going to do?"

Shane purses his lips as he thinks. "We have the advantage of surprise. Michael doesn't seem to know we're here."

"True."

"And that's a colossal advantage. Many wars have been won thanks to the element of surprise. And really, we have a Trojan horse situation going on here. Are you familiar?"

"I think so, yeah," Rebecca says. "Soldiers snuck into Troy, hidden in the cavity of a huge wooden horse, right?"

"That's right," Shane replies. "You're a bright one. I'm a military history buff, but I don't expect everyone to share my passion for the subject. I'm impressed you know that."

"James likes military history, too. I think I saw a documentary about Troy with him at one point. Or maybe it was a movie…"

"Right. So staying hidden until we're ready to make our move is our best play. We might just be able to save your girl if we play our cards right."

"Do you really think so?" Rebecca asked. "I've been so worried about her for a while now. This guy is bad news."

"So, all that talk about how you could see his love for her…?"

"A negotiation tactic."

"I see," Shane confirmed.

"So much for that tactic," Rebecca added. "It didn't work."

"Hey, now," Shane said. "Don't be so hard on yourself. This isn't over yet. You stalled him long enough for us to sneak in here. And that might just make all the difference. Give yourself some credit. You did good, kid."

Rebecca smiled. Now Shane really reminded her of her Uncle Bob. He'd always called her kid.

As if he just remembered something important, Shane reached into his pants pocket and pulled out a small notepad and pencil. "I almost forgot!" he said.

Rebecca raised her brows. "What are you going to do with that, my friend?"

"It helps me think," Shane explained. "Like I said, I'm old school. Back in the Marines, I had to make notes and sketch things out. We didn't have the fancy supercomputers they do these days. It taught me well. Even now, when I have a problem to figure out, this puppy helps me do it."

He held the notebook out in front of him. Its yellow paper cover was tattered from wear and tear. Rebecca was intrigued. She thought that Shane just might know what he was talking about.

"I guess that's what we'll have to do if we want to save Amelia and make it out alive," she said.

"What? Sketch out a plan?"

"You, yes," she continued. "And me, well, I'll need to figure out what skills, abilities, and talents I bring to the table that are relevant here."

"That's the spirit."

"Back to that Trojan horse thing," Rebecca said. "How do you see that playing out in our case. We didn't have the luxury of planning before we hopped in here. We don't have weapons or armor like the Trojan soldiers."

"Yeah, but that doesn't mean we can't make this work," Shane said. "I'm older than dirt, and I believe in my ability to make myself useful."

Rebecca laughed. "Nonsense."

"Anyway, the Trojans waited, then attacked when the enemy least expected it, from within their walls. I'd say our mission is similar. We lay low until we know we have the upper hand. We want Michael to let his guard down."

"And you think we can do that? Just the two of us?" she asked.

"If someone shows up to help, the more, the merrier," Shane replied. "But we can't wait around. We'll assume it's just the two of us. We'll wait and watch for an opportunity. The guy has to sleep at some point."

"Sleep?" Rebecca asked, her eyes widening. "We're going to wait that long?"

"Maybe."

"I'm going to have to pee," she said softly.

Shane smiled. "Ma'am, this is war. There's no shame in bodily functions on the battlefield. You do what you need to do."

Rebecca smiled back. She appreciated Shane's

sensibilities. She might just have to pee on the battlefield. She'd had entirely too much water and wine over lunch to hold it until nighttime. More importantly, though, she wondered if Amelia could survive that long without seeing a doctor. Shane could tell what she was thinking.

"I'm worried about her, too," he said. "She didn't look good by the time he put her in the cab. I don't have any wise words of encouragement in that regard. We'll do our very best. But we have to be smart about it. We're only human, after all."

Rebecca nodded. She knew it was true. She kicked herself for not intervening sooner. She knew her friend was in trouble with Michael. She should have intervened. She should have told James more about the situation. She should have done something. *Anything*.

"I feel like this is all my fault," Rebecca said. "I didn't do enough."

"Now you're talking nonsense," Shane said. 'I recommend you stop that, soldier. It isn't good for morale."

"I'm serious," she replied, though she smiled at Shane's war references. "I knew things were bad. Damn, damn, damn."

Before Shane could speak to reassure her further, the truck took a sudden left turn onto a dirt road. Michael drove slower than he had on the two-lane highway, but still too fast for the condition of the minor road. Dirt billowed up in plumes, settling down over the bed and making Shane and Rebecca cough. Their eyes watered from all the sediment flying around.

"Stay down," Shane whispered.

Rebecca nodded.

"Get up against the side of the bed and make yourself perfectly still. Don't do anything that would draw attention to yourself."

Rebecca nodded again, making her body long and thin against one side of the truck bed. She hugged a wheel well and stayed still, just like Shane had instructed. He did the same on the other side. They'd be seen if anyone walked by, but it's possible they could evade detection from nothing more than a quick glance in the rearview mirror.

They didn't have a better option. They had to hope and pray that whatever Michael was doing, it wouldn't bring him back there.

12

———

A Year Prior, Back Then
Las Vegas, Nevada

As Michael fondled Amelia's naked, bruised body on the bathroom vanity, his erection pushing against her hungrily, she found herself a million miles away. Strangely enough, she found herself thinking about her ex-boyfriend, Troy. There were memories of their time together just below the surface of her consciousness. She had tried desperately to bury them, but to no avail. Once, she had been injured and vulnerable with Troy, her body having taken a beating of a different kind.

It had come on the heels of the single happiest month of Amelia's life. She and Troy had lived together then, and they were completely in love with each other. They'd talked about getting married. Amelia had fully intended to say yes when he popped the question. She'd envisioned the day countless times. They had been taking it slow, which was fine. There had been no rush. Their days had been spent doing typical domestic things-- going to work, cleaning the house, going out to eat on their days off, and all manner of other regular life rituals that made them who they were as individuals and as a couple. There had been a beauty in their routines. Amelia hadn't been bored. Not back then. Quite the opposite. She had been genuinely fulfilled and content.

As she smelled Michael's aftershave and closed her eyes from her position on the vanity, she could clearly remember the day that she had found out she was pregnant. It had been the springtime prior, less than a year before.

The flowers around Rosemary Run had been in bloom that day, just like Amelia. The world had felt hopeful and full to the brim with possibility. Her cycle previously like clockwork each month, Amelia quickly suspected that something was up when she went a week beyond her scheduled period. She hadn't told anyone about her suspicions, preferring instead to keep the news between her and Troy. She had known she'd want to keep her pregnancy quiet until after the first trimester. Amelia had seen and heard about too many early term miscarriages to feel confident about spreading the word. She had known it would crush her if she told her friends, family, and co-workers about a pregnancy and later had to tell them she'd lost the baby. So, instead, she had kept mum on the subject.

On the eighth day past her missed period, Amelia had driven to the neighboring town of Sweet Balm Bay and purchased a pregnancy test from a chain drugstore.

Nonchalantly, she had paid for the test, then asked to use their restroom. Surrounded by white walls and nondescript metal dividers, Amelia had peed on the stick and waited patiently until two lines had shown up, strong and bright as day. Positive. *Pregnant!* She had nearly knocked her head against one of the metal dividers when she'd jumped up and down so enthusiastically.

She had been positively thrilled. Amelia had believed her life was on the right track, and that she and Troy belonged together. She'd wanted a baby to nurture and love. She'd known Troy would be an amazing dad. There had been no doubt about that whatsoever. She'd wanted the three of them to be a happy little family. She'd closed her eyes in that chain drugstore bathroom stall and said a prayer of thanks to the heavens for making her a mommy. She'd never felt more grateful than for the gift of new life growing inside her.

When she'd returned to her car, she immediately called Troy. It had been late morning then, and he wouldn't have been finished with his work day until evening. They had made plans to eat dinner together at the Brick House Cafe in downtown Rosemary Run. Amelia could hardly wait to see her love and tell him the wonderful news. She had gone home and picked out a special dress to wear for the occasion. It had been pastel pink with a large rose adornment on one of the shoulder straps. She could still remember how it felt to slide the fabric over her belly. It had seemed surreal to think that a baby was growing in there. It had thrilled and delighted Amelia to no end. She had looked forward to feeling Troy's big, warm hands on her belly, lovingly tending to her and their child. He was a protector. He had made that clear. Amelia had known that he was just the type of man she wanted to spend her life with.

When she'd told him that evening under the twinkling lights of downtown, Troy had been over the moon. He'd wanted to stand and announce the big news to everyone present. It had been all he could do to hold himself back. He'd felt like shouting, dancing, and clapping. But Amelia had wanted to keep things quiet, so Troy had agreed to honor her wishes. He'd taken her hands into his and told her how much he loved her and what a fantastic mother she'd be. The evening had been everything the two of them could have wished for. The days and weeks that followed had been just as magical. Ultrasound photos had been clipped to the refrigerator, baby clothes had begun to fill the closet in the spare bedroom, and baby names had been discussed during pillow talk each night. The parents-to-be had chosen the name Bella for a baby girl, an Italian word for beautiful in a nod to Amelia's Italian heritage. A baby boy would have been named Ambrose, after Troy's dad.

It hadn't been until nearly four weeks later that Amelia's hopes and dreams came crashing down. The tragedy had befallen her when she woke up one Tuesday morning covered in blood. There had been so much red on the couple's white sheets that it looked like a murder scene. Essentially, it had been exactly that. Amelia had known the moment she'd laid eyes on the stains and felt the wet warmth on her legs that her precious baby was no more. She had been having a miscarriage. As a nurse, she had also known that it was too late to try and save the baby. There had been too much blood. No fetus could have survived. Amelia and Troy had been utterly devastated. The memory so powerful, so all encompassing, that it came forcing its way into Amelia's mind as she tried to delay Michael's advances.

The day of the miscarriage, after Amelia had been checked out and cleaned up by her obstetrician, she and Troy had returned home with empty hands and empty hearts. They hadn't known what to do with themselves. It would be a long time before they'd make love again, and never like before. But Troy had cared for Amelia in a way she'd never forget. For days after she lost the baby, she had felt frozen and numb. Troy had seen her naked, her distended baby bump hollow. She had been ashamed for him to see her body that way. She had felt useless. Like a faulty woman who had failed at the one biological mandate set out for her. Other women could make babies. Why couldn't she?

Troy hadn't seen Amelia the same way she'd seen herself. When she had sat staring at the bathroom floor, he'd lovingly helped her into the tub and sponged her skin gently. He'd taken time off work to take care of her. Even though Troy had been grieving the loss of their child himself, he had focused all of his attention on Amelia. She had felt safe with him. She'd known it was safe to show him her injured, broken body and to let him observe its suffering, then later its healing. With Michael and the bruises Amelia bore now, she didn't feel the same loving care. The difference between the two experiences was troubling.

"Um," Amelia began, thinking about what she could

say to make Michael stop. "I'm not feeling my best," she tried. "I'm all sore for some reason."

She wouldn't have had to tell Troy that she wasn't feeling her best. He would have immediately noticed any bruises on her body. He would have rushed to her, asking what was wrong and what he could do to help her. Amelia began to think that maybe she had given up on the relationship with Troy too soon.

She knew she'd been running from the pain of the miscarriage when she'd broken things off with him. He hadn't wanted their partnership to end. The day she'd told him she was leaving, he'd gotten down on one knee in the backyard and proposed. He'd picked out a ring months before, but had been saving it for just the right time. He'd said he hadn't wanted her to think that he was only proposing because she'd been pregnant, and that he'd bought the ring before the pregnancy test. She should have believed him. She should have let him help her continue to heal. She should have given them a chance to heal together.

Michael grunted, his hands now working feverishly to loosen his belt. He kissed Amelia's neck hard, causing both pain on her bruised skin and what felt like it might develop into a new kind of ecstasy. When his belt swung open, he shrugged his pants off and kicked them across the bathroom floor. In his boxer briefs, Amelia could finally get a good look at his body. It was exquisite. His muscles were tighter and coiled more densely than any man she'd been with. Michael looked like a legitimate work of art, as if he'd been chiseled by a sculptor tasked with creating the perfect man.

Becoming more turned on, Amelia wasn't sure she wanted him to stop.

"Can I make you feel better?" Michael asked.

So, he had heard her. He didn't slow down, though. Michael pushed himself between Amelia's legs, wrapped her thin limbs around his body, then picked her up and carried her to the bed. He wasn't exactly rough, but he wasn't tender either. He slammed himself on top of her, entering her with his full force. No foreplay. No caressing. No asking what she wanted or needed. He seemed aware of her right to choose what she did with her own body, but only vaguely. That clearly wasn't his primary concern.

"Take me," Amelia said through gritted teeth.

She couldn't decide whether she wanted Michael Bell or feared him, so she chose to go along with things and see what happened. She could stand the pain. And maybe, she'd have a chance to experience a new kind of pleasure.

"Oh, I will," he said. "I'm going to take you, alright. I know you want me."

"I do," she replied.

Was it a lie? Amelia wasn't quite sure. She told her body to hold on for the ride and to bring her whatever good feelings it was capable of.

As Michael thrust and pumped, she thought back to *Fifty Shades of Grey*. What was it that Christian Grey did to make Anastasia so wild with desire? Amelia remembered that belts, restraints, gags, and even hot candle wax had been involved. Christian had taken things slow at first, slapping Anastasia's buttocks and binding her hands above her head while she was blindfolded. He got rougher as she became more comfortable with the unconventional situation. If Amelia's memory served her right, that had been what made the story so intriguing. Anastasia had been open to experimentation, but Christian let her move at her own pace. Michael wasn't so accommodating.

Maybe he had been accommodating before… if they'd had sex. Had they? Was this their first time? If so, Amelia wished Michael had tried to romance her a bit more. He was a sexy man, but there had been no romancing. Very little lead in. And virtually no thought of what she liked. Amelia hated to think this way, but what if her bruises were from rough sex with Michael? Is that what had happened to her body? She shuddered to think that sex could hurt so much. And she still wondered why she couldn't remember where her injuries had come from. If the bruises had come from rough sex, had she enjoyed it while it was happening? Is that why Michael wanted her to wear a revealing dress? Was he proud of the marks on her body? Were they a result of his own pleasure?

The most alarming question stung like poison on a dagger. Had Amelia consented? She had been drunk on the night she met Michael. Maybe high. She had chosen to put those substances into her body. She had a vague memory of him refilling her glass and encouraging her to get wasted, but it wasn't like he had forced her. Or had he? Is this how Anastasia had felt? The thoughts blurred and whizzed in Amelia's mind. She had considered herself so sophisticated and savvy. Yet the predicament Amelia found herself in wasn't one that a sophisticated or savvy woman would encounter. No, a savvy woman would have turned and walked away the moment Michael walked into that bar. For that matter, a savvy woman would have remained in a relationship with Troy Weeks. She would have stayed at the home they'd shared and faced their pain together. She would have said yes when Troy proposed. How had things gone so terribly wrong?

Tears ran down Amelia's cheek as Michael did his business. At that point, Amelia couldn't think of a better way to describe it. He tossed her around the bed like a rag doll. His facial expression brought to mind that of a tiger, his mouth fixed tightly around the neck of an impala as it watched the life slowly drain from the helpless animal. When Michael went to the bathroom then returned with his belt, Amelia finally saw her suspicions confirmed.

"You like it rough, don't you?" he asked as he fastened the belt around her wrists and tied them to the headboard.

The same sunlight that had seemed so friendly earlier now shone on what could only be considered a tragedy in Amelia's life. She said nothing as he used a tie from the draperies to bind her ankles. It was the makeshift gag made from the silk shirt she'd been wearing that made her turn and look longingly at the phone on the bedside table. If only she had used her voice when she'd had a chance. If she'd woken up sooner or if the front desk clerk had been less chatty, Amelia could have called her mom. Or Rebecca. Or someone-- *anyone*-- who could help.

13

Present Day
Rosemary Run, California

Within a few minutes after turning off the main highway and onto the dirt road, Michael's truck slowed to a crawl, then stopped. Shane and Rebecca couldn't tell where they were. They didn't dare move and risk being seen. All they could do was listen. Michael turned off the engine, then opened the door and stepped out. He paused and spit before he walked away. The sound of him gathering the contents of his sinuses and hawking them onto the ground was disgusting. It reaffirmed for Rebecca the belief that Michael wasn't nearly as charming as Amelia had claimed.

"Yuck," she mouthed, even though no one could see her.

Rebecca figured Shane had the same reaction, although he was probably less disgusted than she was. As a

Marine, he'd probably seen plenty of gross things. All of his battlefield talk virtually guaranteed it.

They continued to listen as Michael's shoes crunched twigs and flattened dry grass. It seemed like he had walked a good distance from the truck by the time his footsteps fell silent. Probably twenty feet or more. He stood quietly, a pair of birds calling to each other in the distance. Leave it to the wildlife to fill the void. And then, another man's voice could be heard.

"Any trouble?" the man asked.

His voice was gruff and deep. Rough, too. He sounded like a big guy. Maybe a body guard of some sort.

"Nothing I couldn't handle," Michael replied.

"What's that supposed to mean?"

Michael spit again. What was up with all the spitting? Shane and Rebecca both noticed. Maybe Michael was nervous. It wasn't immediately obvious who had the upper hand between the two men. Michael had always seemed like such an alpha personality to Rebecca. What if he wasn't the top of the food chain? That would be an interesting development.

"No need to concern yourself," Michael said. "It's handled."

The other man paused, then grunted his acceptance. "Fine," he mumbled. "It's out back."

Branches cracked again as the men moved. After a few steps, they stopped.

"What's with your woman?" the big man asked. "She asleep?"

Michael spit again.

How strange, Rebecca thought. It must be a tell. A nervous tic. She made a mental note. They could use this.

"Something like that," Michael said.

The big man didn't hesitate now. "Sounds to me like you aren't ready for this," he said, his voice strong and sure.

"Not so," Michael replied. "Forget about her. I have it under control. Are you going to show me the motorhome, or what? You promised me a motorhome."

"It might be out of service," the big man said.

"Fuck you, Byers," Michael said. "That isn't funny. I already paid."

Rebecca and Shane heard something slammed up against metal, then dirt being pounded. It sounded like a scuffle had broken out. They both wanted desperately to take a look and find out what was going on, but they didn't dare move and show themselves.

"Now I know you're out of control," the big man-- presumably Byers-- said. "What do you think you're doing using my name like that. You should know better."

"You're right," Michael said, his voice strained.

It sounded like Byers might have had him by the throat. Unable to resist any longer, Rebecca rolled towards Shane and whispered.

"I think one of us should take a look. We might need to identify this guy to the police later," she said.

Shane nodded. "Agreed. Stay down. I'll do it."

Rebecca rolled back against her side of the truck bed while Shane raised himself up enough to get a quick glance. First, Shane tried to see the men from the reflection in the back window of the truck. No luck. The angle was wrong. He'd have to actually raise his head above the edge of the bed, risking being seen. It was a necessary risk though, no question about that. Slowly, Shane propped himself up high enough to get a look. When he saw the men, he studied them carefully, methodically cataloging the details.

"What do you see?" Rebecca whispered.

Like a prairie dog retreating back into its hole, Shane whipped his head down and resumed his position on the side of the truck bed. "Byers looks treacherous," he said in a hush. "That guy looks like a criminal if I ever saw one. Gang tattoos and all."

"Gang tattoos?"

"Yeah," Shane said. "I couldn't make out the details from this far away, but we aren't dealing with a nice guy. Michael's scared of him."

"How can you tell?"

"His body language screams it. I'll tell you more later. We need to stay quiet."

Rebecca nodded her understanding. The pair waited and listened some more.

"Sorry, man," Michael said.

Any pretense of equal footing between the two men was gone. Michael was, in fact, lower on the food chain than Byers.

"I mean it," Michael said. "I'm sorry. Will you let me take the motor home like we planned, please? I need to ditch this truck. I can't be out on the roads in it."

"Why should I?" Byers asked. "Why should I believe anything you say?"

"Because I won't be able to do the job if you don't

help me. I've got to get off grid. They'll be looking for me."

"Who?"

"It's better if you don't know. But I'm running out of time. Please, the motor home?"

Silence fills the air for what feels to Shane and Rebecca like an unusually long time. For a few minutes, they can't tell whether Michael and Byers have tiptoed away, or if the big man is still considering what he should do. Finally, the jingle of keys could be heard.

"It's around back," Byers says. "Don't disappoint me."

"No, sir," Michael replied. "I won't let you down."

Michael's footsteps could be heard shuffling through the dry grass.

"Hey!" Byers called.

Rebecca and Shane both stiffened. For a second, they thought maybe they'd been seen.

"Yeah?" Michael asked.

"I don't care if you're a big shot in Las Vegas. You're on my territory now. You had better remember that."

"I hear you loud and clear," Michael said, then resumed his trek toward the back of the property.

Rebecca hadn't seen the place, so she had no idea what the scenery was like. A padlock on a chain link fence could be heard clanking against the metal post as Michael passed through. Shane knew they were parked in front of what appeared to be a junkyard. There was a small mobile home in the center that seemed to be an office. When he'd looked, a mangy yellow dog had stood guard in an open doorway. A metal fence surrounded the back section of the property and appeared to go back quite a ways past beaten up cars, trucks, motor homes, and busses. The whole place was run down and dilapidated. Like an abandoned graveyard of sorts, filled with dead and dying vehicles. It was a far cry from what he imagined Michael's living standards were in Vegas.

Relieved that the men were further away for the moment, Rebecca felt comfortable enough to speak again.

"We should check on Amelia," she said.

Shane reached a hand out and placed it on her forearm. "Not so fast," he said.

"But she's in desperate need of help," she said. "I was thinking... Maybe we should make a move right now. One of us could jump into the driver's seat and drive away before Michael returns."

"Of course, I thought about that, too," he said. "It's too risky right now. Byers is close. That man surely has a weapon. By the time we start the engine up, he'll have it trained on us and he won't hesitate to shoot. We're on his property, so he might even have a right to shoot. He could make a good case of that, anyway. So where would that leave us?"

"I guess you're right," Rebecca conceded.

"I know you're eager to help your friend," Shane said. "Patience."

Before Rebecca could say anything else, they heard heavy footsteps headed their way.

"Be quiet!" Shane exclaimed in a whisper.

Rebecca nodded. They could tell the footsteps were heavier than Michael's. It was Byers, no doubt come to see what was happening with Amelia. Rebecca had mixed feelings about this development. She was terrified of being found by this big, aggressive men. Standing up to him wouldn't be like standing up to a man like Michael. She'd still do it out of principal, but she knew things wouldn't go well if she did. On the other hand, though, he had asked about Amelia. Maybe he was genuinely concerned about her. Maybe he even had the decency to get her some help. It didn't seem outside the realm of possibility.

Shane quietly reached one foot to Rebecca's and touched his toe to hers. It was a gesture of comfort that let her know she wasn't in this alone. She greatly appreciated it. She closed her eyes as Byers got closer and closer, willing her body to remain calm so that she could stay quiet. She felt so helpless there. And she hated it.

In her mind, Rebecca went over the various ways the next moments could play out. Byers could notice her and Shane hiding in the back, decide they were a threat, and shoot them in cold blood. She wouldn't be surprised to learn that Byers knew how to dispose of a body. He'd probably disposed of more than one or two in his time. She'd been a missing person. Her murder might never be solved. There would be little to tie her to this place, wherever it was. James might never find out what had happened to her.

If Byers noticed Rebecca and Shane, but didn't think they were a threat, perhaps they could claim that Michael had kidnapped them. That idea might have legs. They could point out how he had attacked Amelia, and claim that he was out of control. Byers had seemed inclined to discredit Michael and turn against him. Could that actually work? It sounded promising until Rebecca realized that they'd probably heard too much for Byers to ever let them go. He'd have to kill them to keep his business dealings secret. *Damn*, she thought.

Scenario number three, perhaps the most likely, saw Byers focusing on Amelia and never noticing Shane and Rebecca in the back. He'd probably approach the truck from the front, his eyes turned toward Amelia as he attempted to determine whether she was really just asleep. By the time he noticed that more was going on, he'd have entered the cab where he'd be less likely to look into the bed of the truck. If that happened, Shane and Rebecca might go undetected. Byers might call for help for Amelia, or at a minimum, drop her off at a hospital. That would be great for Amelia, but what would it mean for Shane and Rebecca? How would they get out and away from Michael? And if they did, how would they get back to civilization and safety? Rebecca estimated that they were at least ten miles out of town. That would be a long walk in this mountainous terrain. She guessed it was doable. She was in good physical shape. Shane looked like he was, too. And maybe they'd get a phone signal at some point during the walk back to town.

What Rebecca really wished would happen involved James showing up, sirens blaring, to rescue her. In that fantasy, James would have plenty of backup. A stream of cop cars would follow him. He'd arrest Michael and Byers, and take them into custody. Then he'd call for EMTs who would treat Amelia on the scene and take her to the hospital when they were sure she was stable enough to transport. Other police officers would scour the scene, collecting evidence to shut down whatever territory and business dealings Michael and Byers were involved in. A local judge would prosecute the criminals. And the residents of Rosemary Run could get back to their regular lives.

As Byers stepped just feet from the truck, Rebecca held her breath. Whether one of her imagined scenarios was about to play out or something entirely different, she and Shane would soon find out.

14

A Year Prior, Back Then
Las Vegas, Nevada

When Michael was finished with Amelia, he gathered his clothes and quickly put them back on. He didn't so much as glance at her bruised body, used and discarded on the bed. Embarrassed, she covered herself with a sheet and stared out the window. She hoped Michael would finally leave her alone. She needed space to collect herself and to get in touch with someone who would come to her aid.

"Be downstairs in fifteen minutes," he said. "Wear the dress."

He slammed the door hard as he left the condo.

Just fifteen minutes, Amelia thought. Scarcely enough time to make herself presentable and figure out a way to hide her bruises. *About that phone call…*

Wincing, Amelia turned back to the bedside table and picked up the receiver. Until she realized the danger in doing so. Had it been a 9 or a 1 that she was supposed to dial for an outside line? If she dialed incorrectly and got the front desk clerk, the chipper woman would call her Mrs. Bell and tell her Michael had arrived in the lobby. He'd hear his name, and he'd know Amelia was trying to contact someone. Amelia doubted he'd like that. He was waiting on her so that they could go somewhere. She didn't know where, but she knew she shouldn't keep him waiting. He'd want her available for whenever he decided she could be of some use to him. Amelia set the phone back down, her heart breaking at how close, yet also how far help was.

Think, she told herself. *What can be done?*

No matter how much she tried to look on the bright side or how much she'd tried to enjoy sex with Michael, Amelia was unhappy. She thought she might have experienced the best sex of her life. Instead, it had been the worst. She had been scared with her eyes covered and her limbs tied. Michael's rough touch under those conditions had felt bad. No pleasure had entered the equation. She'd sucked in her sobs and held back her tears in the hopes that Michael would finish quickly and let her go. In the end, it had been the worst sex of her life.

A cold chill went up Amelia's spine as she huddled under the thin sheet. Everything hurt. She knew it was warm in the room, but her body was in shock. The combination of the physical pain and the emotional distress was causing her to feel cold. Sometimes, Amelia shifted into nurse mode when it wasn't helpful for her to do so. When in this mode, she looked at everything clinically, with a detached perspective. It was a survival instinct. But it only served to delay her coming to the realization that she was in trouble. She found herself detached from reality now, shivering and afraid.

Time was ticking. Amelia wasn't sure how many minutes had passed since Michael had left the condo, but she knew he'd be looking for her soon. Before she could gather herself and stand, a knock sounded from the front door. She hadn't even been out of the bedroom to see where the door was, but she could hear it well enough to tell that the knocking was directed at this condo.

A sinking feeling took hold of her stomach. She thought about the large man who had grabbed her by the throat. How had she falled into his grips in the first place? Had Michael given Amelia to the other man for him to use her, too? That was a stretch, but not much would surprise Amelia at this point. She was finally coming to terms with the fact that Michael wasn't a good guy. He wasn't the man of her dreams. More like the horrors from her nightmares. But she couldn't let on. Not a soul could know. She had to play the part of a loving, happy wife until she could find a way to get free... for good. Amelia knew Michael could find her anywhere. He had that ability, no doubt.

"Who is it?" Amelia called, unsure whether the person at the door could hear her.

"Room service!" a man's voice returned.

Amelia shook. She had forgotten about the bacon and eggs that Michael ordered. She couldn't eat a thing right then if she tried. She was too disgusted to stomach any food or drink. Not even wine sounded good. More pressing than whether or not to eat was her worry that it wasn't actually room service out there. Could it be the big man? Was he there to use and abuse her now that Michael had his fill?

"No, thank you," Amelia tried, trembling.

She could tell that her voice was feeble. She wondered if the man could tell.

"But I have an order here for this room. It's bacon, eggs, toast, and orange juice. Looks delicious."

"I didn't order anything," she said. "No, thank you."

There was silence. Amelia considered opening the door. The man had sounded friendly. And he had sounded younger than the big man she remembered from her boozy night. It felt dangerous to open that door though. And every second that went by without her showing up downstairs could cause Amelia all sorts of trouble with Michael.

"I'm not hungry," she said. "Please, leave me be."

Her voice broke on the last word. The man would know something was wrong with her now. Amelia covered her mouth with the sheet, still shaking, as she waited to see if the man would go away.

"Ma'am," he began after another minute, "are you okay?"

Amelia cursed the man, and herself. She shouldn't have said anything. Maybe then he would have simply left the tray in front of the door. She couldn't imagine how any employee of this hotel could actually help her without tipping off Michael. Therefore, she wanted them all to leave her alone. She needed to focus on keeping Michael unsuspecting of her desire to get away from him. It was a delicate task fraught with potential landmines.

She swallowed hard. "Fine. I'm just… I'm running late."

There. That had sounded reasonable. At least, Amelia hoped so. She stood carefully, wincing with pain but managing to hold her cries in. She wrapped the sheet around her body, tucking it gently under one arm. She was bent over in front of a dresser when she heard the distinctive sound of the door being unlocked. She froze. Like a deer in headlights, her terror was too great to make her body move. She was in too much pain to move quickly, anyway.

Sheepishly, a gangly young man entered the condo-- or hotel room or whatever this was-- a plastic tray with a silver dish balanced on one arm. He appeared to be in his early twenties. He was much younger than Amelia. He was all fresh faced and enthusiastic, his reddish-blonde hair tied in a man bun on the back of his head. He held his free hand up in front of him to indicate that he wasn't a threat.

"Ma'am, I'm sorry for the intrusion," he said. "It's just… well, you sounded… something in your voice made me decide I should…"

His face fell as he stepped closer and caught a glimpse of Amelia's bruised neck and shoulders.

"Oh, my…" he stammered.

Amelia shook her head, unable to find words. She remained frozen, as if her feet were stuck to the floor. She wasn't sure what to do or say. Her fifteen minutes were nearly up.

The young man set the tray down on the coffee table of the living room that Amelia could now see from her vantage point. He then raised his other hand in the air in a classic pose that said he surrendered. Or maybe it was just so Amelia had a clear view of his hands. He moved slowly, not wanting to spook her. He could tell she was in distress. He feared for her safety. He probably saw the situation more clearly than Amelia did herself.

"Ma'am," he continued. "I'm going to lock the chain on this door so no one joins us in here until we're sure we're ready. Okay?"

Amelia nodded, her eyes wild with panic.

"I'm Jake," he said as he fastened the chain, then turned back to face her. "Jake Webber. I work here."

She nodded again, her head the only thing she could move.

"Ma'am, it looks like you're in some trouble," he said. "Can I call someone?"

Amelia's mind raced. There was still the problem of the perky front desk clerk and Michael being there to overhear. She couldn't call anyone from the hotel phone. It was too risky.

"I can't," she mumbled.

Jake lowered his brows. He had a calm presence, as if he'd been trained to work with people in a panicked state like Amelia was. She could recognize that from a clinical perspective, yet she didn't identify with it emotionally. She still didn't realize how severe her level of trauma actually was.

"I believe you can," Jake said. "I can dial the phone for you, if you like." He moved to pick up the receiver of a phone on a small table beside the living room sofa. It was the same model as the one in the bedroom.

"No!" Amelia shouted. "I can't. I have to get dressed. My... someone is waiting for me downstairs. I..."

Jake nodded as if he understood exactly what she was saying. And what she was not saying. "I get it," he said, finishing her sentence. "You don't want to keep him waiting."

"Yes, that's right," Amelia replied. "I need to get dressed."

"Okay," Jake said, his plush, wiry beard rippling as he spoke. He looked like a perfect mountain man. If Amelia had been in a better frame of mind, she would have asked where he was from. "What if you told me the number and I dialed while you were getting dressed?" he continued. "We'd save time that way."

Amelia shook her head. "I can't. I wish I could, but I can't."

Jake frowned. This was turning out to be more difficult than he had expected. At least, he had her talking. That was progress. He'd take it. He could tell she was in trouble and he wanted to help.

"Ma'am, I think it's important that we call someone. I want to call someone for you. Please. Humor me if that's what it takes. I'm an overeager young man who wants to do right by the world so it will do right by me. Will you let me make a phone call on your behalf?"

Amelia considered it. She wanted to let him call for help. She wanted so badly to speak to her mom or Rebecca. At this point, she was beginning to wish she could talk to Troy. But it felt too risky. Maybe, though, she could gather a few bits of information from Jake and still make it downstairs in time to keep from setting Michael off.

"How about this?" she asked.

"Anything, ma'am," Jake replied.

"I have to get dressed…"

"To get downstairs in time," he replied. "I know."

"Right. But what if I asked you a few questions while I do?"

"Of course," he said. "You name it."

Amelia nodded, a small smile landing on her lips. She couldn't wait to solve some of the mystery surrounding her situation. She backed slowly into the bedroom, careful not to lose the sheet that was covering her body.

"I'll sit on the sofa here and listen for your questions," Jake said as he slowly sat down. "We can talk through the closed door, if you want. I'll be able to hear you."

"It can stay open," Amelia replied.

She trusted Jake. Like, really trusted him. Not in the crossed signals kind of way she'd thought she'd trusted Michael. She could tell Jake was an upstanding, trustworthy young man. She felt completely at ease with him. Suddenly, a pang of sadness hit Amelia as she realized that she would have liked for her son to grow up to be like Jake. If her body hadn't rejected and destroyed his tiny one, of course. It was at that very moment when something startling became clear to Amelia. It might have been obvious to an outsider who'd heard the depressing story, but in her mind, it was brand new. She let out a loud, heaving sob as the realization settled over her, heavy and overwhelming.

"Ma'am?" Jake asked in response. "Are… are you okay?"

"No! I'm not," Amelia sputtered. "I deserve this!"

"Whoa, now," Jake said, his voice carrying throughout the space. "That can't possibly be true."

"I do!" Amelia wailed, finding her voice for the first time in a long time. "I let… My… It was my fault…"

"No, no, no," Jake said. "Nothing you've done could be bad enough for you to deserve this. No way. I don't believe it. Not for a minute."

Amelia looked up at the heavens and shook her fist. "Why?" she pleaded. "Why me? Why us?"

Her sobs became even heavier as she fell to the floor, the sheet billowing around her. What had happened to her wasn't fair. It was, in fact, cruel. And completely devastating in every sense of the word. She hadn't known how she could go on with the pain she'd felt inside. Now, the pain on the outside of her body was nearly as intense. She had orchestrated all of this. Maybe not consciously, but with her poor decisions, she had made it such that something like this would happen, even if she hadn't known exactly how the new pain would manifest. She had sought it out. She believed she deserved it.

Ignoring the plan to stay on the sofa, Jake rushed into the bedroom in an effort to come to Amelia's aid.

"Oh, ma'am," he said as he crouched down beside her. He covered one of Amelia's exposed legs to give her privacy. "I'm here for you. You don't know me, and that's probably a little weird for you, but I'm right here. What can I do?"

Amelia yelled and screamed, her emotional pain

pouring out. When she'd expelled the tip of it from her being, she flung herself against Jake's kind shoulder. "I…" she began, her face soaking wet with tears.

"Go on," Jake said. "Get it out. You can tell me."

She looked up at his kind eyes. This young man's mama had raised him right.

"I… My baby died," Amelia screamed. "I lost my baby… Mine and Troy's. My baby is dead. Gone! And I lost *him*… the only man I've ever truly loved because I pushed him away while I was busy running from the pain."

15

Present Day
Rosemary Run, California

Back at Maison du Vin, Marcheline stood flabbergasted as she stared out at the road leading to her property. Michael had sped away so fast that no one had been able to catch up to him. Several people had gotten into cars in pursuit, but none could find him. It was almost as if he'd vanished into thin air. Marcheline wondered how he had been able to successfully elude an entire crowd of people, herself included.

"Ms. Fay," one of the good samaritan men began, "what do we do?"

"I still don't know," she said without hesitation. "I'm sorry, but I don't. Something is very strange about this day. Where are the police? Are they coming?"

A young woman from a few feet away overheard. "I have a police scanner in my car," she offered. "I'll go get it. Maybe we can find out what's keeping our men and women in blue."

"I'll call them again!" someone else shouted.

"Already did," said another. "Dispatch says they're en route."

Marcheline furrowed her brow. Someone must have caused a diversion so Michael could get away with that woman. Amelia is her name, right?"

No one replied to confirm.

"Does anyone here know her?" Marcheline asked. Blank faces looked back at her. "No one?"

"She's familiar," one woman said. "I don't know her name though."

Marcheline shook her head. Where was luck when she needed it? Where was divine intervention. Someone needed to help Amelia, and Marcheline intended to be part of the solution. She'd never be able to live with herself if she stood by idly.

"She's a friend of Rebecca Tatum's," the woman with the police scanner said as she returned with the device in hand. "That was Rebecca she was with. And Rebecca who leaped in the back of that truck."

"Yes, I'd heard her called Rebecca," Marcheline confirmed. "She's Officer James Tatum's wife, yes?"

"That's right."

"He'll want to know that his wife is in danger. How can we get in touch with him?" Marcheline asked.

"I can drive to the police station right now!" the woman responded enthusiastically. "My aunt used to be a dispatcher there. I still know some of the officers and employees."

The woman's silky black hair hung close around her chin. Her clothes were carefully tailored, and she looked ultra neat and put together. Everything about her appearance gave an impression of diligence and reliability. A pair of sunglasses were tucked in the collar of her button-down blouse. She didn't carry a handbag. Maybe she had left one in her car, but Marcheline thought she might be too sensible for such an accessory. Perhaps this woman had been involved in law enforcement or the like herself. She could easily have passed for a whip-smart detective or private investigator.

"Wonderful!" Marcheline replied. "Please, go."

The woman nodded, handing the scanner to Marcheline. "Use this," she said. "It's pretty self explanatory."

Marcheline nodded. "What is your name, miss?"

"Blanca," the woman said. "Blanca Salazar. I'll help you in any way I can, Ms. Fay."

"For that, I'm grateful," Marcheline confirmed. "Thank you. Please tell the staff at the police station that I sent you. Tell them I own Maison du Vin, and that no help has arrived despite multiple calls for assistance."

"Will do."

"And Blanca..." Marcheline added, reaching out and touching the woman's shoulder.

"Yes, Ms. Fay?"

"Please, be careful. I don't like this. There's more going here than the eye sees."

Blanca wanted to chuckle at Marcheline's phrasing, but she didn't. She knew Marcheline was French, and that English was her second language. It was Blanca's second language, too, having been born to Mexican parents. Perhaps, under different circumstances, the two women would have had time to chat and become friends. Right now, they had work to do.

"Understood. I'll be careful," Blanca confirmed. "On my way."

As Blanca headed for her vehicle, Marcheline felt a familiar hand on her shoulder. She turned to see her business associate and close friend, Rande Floyd. His weathered, crooked smile was a sight for sore eyes.

"You alright, Ma'am?" Rande asked, the concern evident in his deep voice.

Rande was Marcheline's right-hand man at Maison du Vin who had recently taken the reins to allow Marcheline a quieter life after years of working herself to the bone. Rande affectionately called her Ma'am. It was his nickname for his dear friend, part token of respect and part good-natured teasing. When he'd first come to work for her, Marcheline had thought it a bit strange. Soon though, she came to appreciate Rande's charm. He was an older cowboy type. Despite his slow drawl, he was incredibly smart. The two had become quite the pair, in both business and their friendship. Not to mention, Rande had helped Marcheline through one of the most difficult times in her life. At this point, Marcheline would have let Rande call her anything he liked.

Rande had been born and raised in Rosemary Run, then had spent two decades in Wyoming working on a cattle ranch. He had married late in life to a younger woman who ended up wanting to put down roots somewhere the kids could grow up knowing their grandparents. When Rande returned to town, Marcheline had been his first stop. He'd heard of the high standards at her winery and knew he wanted to be involved. It took a little convincing, but Marcheline quickly came to understand Rande's charms. In the year since they'd been working together, they had become known as an odd couple in the local business community. On the surface, Rande and Marcheline seemed like opposites, but the differences in their backgrounds only served to benefit their partnership. Rande had a good head on his shoulders. Marcheline relied on him to be the voice of reason and to focus on practicality. He had not disappointed her.

"Rande, my darling!" she exclaimed, relieved to see him. "I thought you were in the winery office today. I didn't call or text because, well, it all happened so fast. I haven't had a chance to."

"I heard a commotion," he said. "I'm here now. Tell me what you need."

"I need to come up with a game plan," she said. "Let's put our heads together. I'll tell you everything I know."

"Okay, then," Rande said. "Is Julien around? He could sure help, too."

Julien Caron was Marcheline's new husband. He was French and a vineyard owner, too. They hadn't been married long, but Julien had folded into Marcheline's business life as effortlessly as he had into her personal one. They'd met at a winemaker conference in San Luis Obispo, California when Julien had been visiting the States from Bordeaux, France. On that precious day, love and romance had shown up when Marcheline least expected it. The happy couple now ran the new Maison du Vin restaurant together while Rande handled day-to-day operations of the winery.

"He made a supply run," Marcheline said. "I'm not sure how soon he'll be back."

Rande nodded. "Bill was nosing around in the winery office not long ago. We can bring him in on this."

Bill Henderson was a former private investigator who Marcheline had hired to help out at the winery. He had started out as her adversary, but had quickly become a trusted friend.

"Yes, Bill would be a big help in this instance," Marcheline confirmed. "Will you get him?"

"Done," Rande said as he pulled out his phone to text Bill.

"I'll call Julien, then let's get together to talk. We'll need to hurry. Others here want to help, too. They're waiting on my direction."

Rande nodded, then gestured towards the road. "Looks like you won't have to call your man, after all," he said.

Julien's large black SUV barreled down the road, then into the parking lot. He was driving much faster than usual. Gravel crunched under his tires.

"What's gotten into him?" Marcheline asked.

"He must've heard that something was happening," Rande replied. "Good man. He intends to be here for you."

Marcheline smiled, despite the worrisome circumstances. She loved her husband, her friends, and her family. Seeing Amelia in harm's way at the hands of a man who claimed to love her had reminded Marcheline of the turmoil that once filled her life and occupied her thoughts. She was grateful for the opportunities she'd had to learn, grow, and move past her pain. Her life was beautiful in every way now. It wasn't perfect, but it was built on solid foundations of meaningful relationships and time well spent. Even though the two women didn't know each other yet, Marcheline wished the same for Amelia. She hoped that someday, Amelia would have a life filled with the same depth and true beauty.

Julien parked his SUV hastily, then practically jumped out of the vehicle to rush to Marcheline. His boots crunched the gravel just as intensely as his tires had.

"My love, are you okay?" he asked his wife as he took her into his arms.

Julien Caron was the picture of rugged French handsomeness. He was tall with dark hair beginning to silver at the temples, calming green eyes, a closely cropped beard, and a crooked smile that made him look like he was always in on a delicious secret.

"I am, my darling," Marcheline replied. "I'm afraid I let an endangered woman down, but I hope there's still time to make up for it."

"Your gun?" Julien asked, his face filled with concern as he felt the weapon in Marcheline's waistband.

Marcheline eyed him. "In time, I'll tell you. I'm still trying to figure it out myself."

Accepting that answer for now, Julien turned to Rande. The two of them had become friends as well.

"Thank you for being here and looking out for our girl," Julien said.

"I'd have done as you say, but I just got out here a few minutes ago," Rande admitted. "No worries though. She's okay, and we're both here now. Bill texted back. He's on the way down from the winery office."

"Good," Marcheline said.

The crowd hung around, as if they didn't want to leave until they knew someone would save Amelia. It was a natural human tendency. They wished to be sure that everyone was okay. Good people wanted that for other good people. Sensing the crowd's interest, Marcheline decided to address them as a group.

"I want to talk to them," she said softly to Julien and Rande.

"Then let's get you up high where they can see you, Ma'am," Rande said.

"The bench!" Julien said, and pointed.

It was the same bench Amelia and Rebecca had sat on a short time before to take a selfie. How sad that it would now be the center of a discussion about how to save them. Marcheline walked quickly toward it, the crowd parting to give her room along the way. Julien and Rande each extended their hand, which Marcheline took as she stepped up onto the seat. When she was up high enough to see over the heads of the people gathered, she found solid footing and began to speak.

"Everyone," she said, "may I have your attention?"

From her vantage point, she saw Bill hurrying down the hill. She waited while he joined them and took his place next to Julien and Rande. Even though they didn't all know what had happened, the Maison du Vin leadership team projected a united front. Julien, Rande, and Bill were at Marcheline's side for whatever was to come. Again, Marcheline thought about how fortunate she was to have the life she did now. Again, her heart broke for poor Amelia. A hush fell over the crowd, their expressions eager.

"For those of you who don't know me," she began, "I'm Marcheline Fay. I own Maison du Vin. This is my husband, Julien Caron, my dearest friend and head of winery operations, Rande Floyd, and another treasured friend and associate, Bill Henderson. Together, the four of us are the leaders at this place of business."

The crowd erupted into applause, surprising Marcheline. She waved her hands appreciatively, then lowered them to signal her desire for quiet. A gentle breeze lifted her dark curls and carried the sweet scent of the restaurant through the air. It was too bad that the connections being made were a result of such a tragic situation. The camaraderie was inspiring. It was needed now more than ever.

"Thank you," Marcheline said. "I've been here, running Maison du Vin for the better part of my life. I came to Rosemary Run after college, and I've grown to love this community and all of you in it. You've welcomed me and my daughter-- and now her husband, their children, and even my parents-- into your town and your hearts. I'm more grateful than I can begin to express."

A few people clapped, and one let out an enthusiastic whistle. Then they quieted down again. Everyone present felt the weight of the matter at hand. They were focused and ready. They were awaiting instructions. They needed a leader, and Marcheline was ready to step up and fill the role.

"Most of you already know why we're gathered here," Marcheline continued. "My heart is heavy, just like I know yours is. Taking deliberate, calculated action will be the salve that mends us all. Let's get started."

16

A Year Prior, Back Then
Las Vegas, Nevada

Jake and Amelia were on the bedroom floor when they heard a clicking from the front door. It was the handle. Someone was trying to get in with a keycard, but the chain Jake had fastened wasn't letting them.

"Oh, God," Amelia said under her breath as she frantically wiped tears from her cheeks. "It's him."

"Who?" Jake asked, quickly realizing exactly who. He knew it before the word had left his mouth. "Oh," he said.

"I'm in trouble now," Amelia said, her face burning hot with a terrible mix of embarrassment, pain, and fear.

The person at the door banged on it loudly. It was clear they intended to enter and that they wouldn't take no for an answer.

"Amelia?"

It was definitely Michael. Amelia was surprised that he knew her name. She wasn't sure he knew or would remember it. That fact illustrated just how sad their relationship was. If it could even be called a relationship in the first place.

"Is that…?" Jake asked.

His eyes were kind, forgiving. Amelia hated to have dragged him into this. She feared he would pay a steep price for getting in Michael's way. Poor Jake didn't deserve that. No one did, but at least Amelia had engaged with Michael. Jake had merely been delivering room service and then decided, out of the goodness of his heart, to help her.

Amelia nodded. "I told you, I had to get downstairs in time. Now he's angry."

"Amelia!" Michael shouted now, his voice booming. He had given up trying to charm her. "Open the damn door."

"Shh," Jake said. "Don't answer him. We can call for help. I'll go to the phone. Security can come."

Amelia shook her head. "You can try," she said. "But it won't matter. This man won't let anything stop him when he sets his mind on something. And he seems to think he's invincible. Maybe he is."

"No one's invincible," Jake said. "I'm going to make the call. Stay quiet."

Jake raised a finger in front of his lips as he stood and walked to the phone on the bedside table. Amelia looked away. She couldn't bring herself to nod and follow his instruction to be quiet. She knew it wouldn't do any good. The chain couldn't be fastened from the outside, so

Michael knew that someone was inside. He surely also knew that someone was Amelia.

"I mean it," Michael said, attempting to control himself.

Amelia thought perhaps someone was out there in the hallway. Maybe knowing that someone was watching made him want to act normal instead of like a raving lunatic. That much was good. At least, he had some sense of social decorum. Amelia could use that to her advantage when they were in public. In fact, staying in public around other people sounded like a good idea. Doing so would probably be her best chance at survival.

Jake picked up the receiver and dialed 0 for the front desk. Amelia closed her eyes, balling her hands into tight fists around the sheet. Anxiety had practically paralyzed her. She listened as the young woman at the front desk picked up. She must have been busy down there, because she immediately put him on hold.

"No! Wait…" Jake said, but it was no use. He was on hold. And Michael had heard his voice.

"Is that a man's voice I hear in there?" Michael asked.

Amelia opened her mouth to answer, but Jake shushed her. He looked at her sternly and shook his head emphatically no. She shrugged her shoulders, as if to say that she had no choice. Her eyes were wild with fear. She figured things would only get worse the longer she put Michael off. She sat up onto her heels, ready to go to the door and let him in.

"Amelia, I swear to God, if you don't open this door right now, I'm breaking it down!"

Amelia jumped with fright. Michael's Southern accent

didn't sound nearly as charming as it had when they met. She looked at the front door, then back at Jake again. She desperately wanted to deescalate the situation. Jake had been so good in helping her calm down. Might he have the same effect on Michael?

Jake held the receiver to his ear. "Come on, hurry up," he said into it.

"Can you do something to calm him down?" Amelia asked. "You seem good at that."

It sounded ridiculous, even to her as she said it. Of course, young Jake couldn't calm Michael down. Amelia figured that no one could. Michael was entitled. He truly believed that everyone and everything should revolve around him. He had no time or patience for any less.

Jake shook his head. "I'm sorry, I don't think so. We need security. If the clerk would just answer."

"Amelia!" Michael roared at the highest volume they'd heard yet.

Jake hung up the phone and tried again. He pressed 0 against the new dial tone, then stared out the window. He was thinking about an escape plan. There had to be a way out. If security didn't get there in time, he and Amelia would be on their own. They'd need to get out of this suite. And if they couldn't, they'd need to hide.

Feeling defeated, Amelia rolled off her heels and settled into a fetal position amongst the sheets which were now bloody from her various sores and wounds. She hadn't examined herself to know for sure, but she thought she was bleeding vaginally from the rough sex. Had Michael torn something inside her? It hurt as if he had. Would he care if he knew? Amelia doubted it.

Suddenly, Michael slammed himself against the door. He had grown tired of waiting and was now working to break the door down, just like he'd promised. He yelled out in a growl as he heaved his body against the door again and again. He was a big man, tall and muscular. It wouldn't take long for him to break the chain.

"Try an outside line," Amelia said to Jake. "Can you call my mom? I know her number. I've wanted to call her all day."

"Your mom?" Jake asked, confused. "How about the police?"

Amelia shook her head. "They won't get here in time, anyway. And I just want to talk to my mom. Don't judge me."

Jake looked at Amelia, perplexed. He continued to hold the phone receiver to his ear. It was ringing, but no one was picking up. "I'm not judging you, believe me. I promise. If you don't hear anything else I say today, please, hear that. You're okay in my book. I mean it."

A hint of relief washed over Amelia's face. It wasn't much, but it meant a lot.

"Okay, so call her," Amelia said as she recited her mom's telephone number out loud.

Michael heard her from outside the door, which was remarkable considering the loud racket he was causing as he body slammed the door.

"I hear you now!" Michael shouted. "Don't screw with me, Amelia, you cunt. Let me in." Then quieter, under his breath, "I'll have this door down within minutes, anyway."

Amelia tried to ignore Michael. She knew she'd be beaten when he got through the door. She also knew she'd be taken away against her will. She didn't even want to think about what would happen to Jake. While she could, she just wanted to call Diane. She wanted to hear her mom's voice, for even a minute. She wanted someone to know she was in trouble.

"Do it! I'm begging you," she said to Jake. "I want my mom to know I'm in trouble. I… I want to hear her voice. We don't have the closest relationship, but I love her. She's my one and only mom, you know?"

Taking a deep, reluctant breath, Jake acquiesced. He took the phone receiver away from his ear, then placed it against his chest while he used the other hand to dial. As an employee, he knew how to get an outside line. What he apparently didn't know was how dangerous Michael Bell was. If Jake had known the extent of the danger they were in, he would have called the police.

"Okay, okay," he said. "Tell me the number again."

Amelia repeated it, careful to enunciate each digit.

"What's her name?"

"Diane. Diane Baker. Tell her it's her daughter, Amelia."

Jake nodded, again looking out the window while he waited for Diane to pick up. He wasn't sure what Amelia hoped to accomplish, other than hearing her mom's voice. He had only just met Amelia, but he wished she'd think more strategically about how to get to safety and take care of herself.

"What do you do?" Jake asked as waited.

"What do you mean?" Amelia asked. "For work?"

"Yeah, I'm just curious," he said.

Michael pounded the door furiously, loosening the

chain with every impact. Jake and Amelia were both surprised the chain had held this long. It must have been some kind of industrial strength device. In Jake's mind, he knew Michael was dangerously angry and that, ideally, they needed an escape plan. Even so, he underestimated the threat. He wouldn't have been idly chatting if he'd had any idea what was going to happen next.

"I'm a pediatric nurse," Amelia said. "I work in a hospital back in my hometown of Rosemary Run."

"Interesting. A nurse, huh? I've heard that town name before," Jake said. "Rosemary Run. Sounds nice."

"I'm not actually from there," Amelia said. "But I've lived there a long time, so I guess it's my adopted home town. Is my mom picking up?"

"She isn't," Jake said as he hung up the phone. "I get voicemail. I'll try her again."

Amelia's heart sank. Talking to Diane was the only thing keeping her going right now. It was the only hope of letting someone who loved her know what was happening. Amelia wasn't sure she remembered Rebecca's number without looking it up. And besides, there wasn't time."

At the door, things got suddenly quiet. No more banging on the door or body slamming it to break it down. Had Michael given up?

"That might be a good sign," Jake said. "Maybe he finally gave up."

Amelia knew that Michael wouldn't have given up that easy. He must have been moving to a plan B. And that wasn't good. It would only serve to solidify his determination. He would get in. Amelia had no doubt about that.

In a flash, Jake's eyes lit up as a voice could be heard on the other end of the phone. "Ms. Baker?" he asked.

"Diane Baker?"

Amelia leaped from the floor, barely keeping herself covered by the sheet. Modesty was the least of her concerns at this point.

"Don't hang up!" Jake said. "I have your daughter here, Amelia. She wants to talk to you."

He beamed as he held the receiver out to Amelia. She took it from him, pressing it to her face. The relief soothed her aching body and spirit. Right now, Amelia's mom was the best medicine. Amelia had been through so much, and not just in Las Vegas. She was tired, beaten down by it all. She didn't want to pretend to be okay any more. She wanted to tell the truth about her pain to the people who loved her. She wanted to let them know how much she cared about them, rather than keep everyone at a distance as a coping mechanism. It wasn't working, anyway.

"Mom?" Amelia said desperately. "Are you there? Is it really you?"

"Good gracious," Diane replied. "What's going on, Amelia? We've been worried sick about you?"

"You have?" Amelia asked. "How did you…?"

"Rebecca called me when you didn't make your flight. She said you'd gone out and never returned to the hotel room. That was three days ago. The longest three days of my life, I might add. The authorities have been looking for you, although since you're an adult band you left of your own volition, they don't seem serious about trying to find you. The detective I talked to at the Las Vegas Police

Department told me you'd turn up when you were ready. Can you believe that?"

Diane was a talker. She rarely let Amelia get a word in edgewise. But Amelia didn't mind. She was just glad to listen right now.

"Three days?" Amelia asked. "Have I really been gone that long?"

In a way, it made sense. The soreness and bruises on her body had an edge to them that only comes after some time has passed. Not to mention, Amelia got the idea that the bruises had come from multiple sessions, or multiple days. As much as she hated to admit it, Amelia now thought maybe Michael had, in fact, slipped some sort of drug into her drink on their first evening together. She had suspected as much. What else could explain the missing time?

"It has," Diane said. "That was Saturday, when you were supposed to fly home. It's Tuesday now. By the way, where on Earth are you?"

"I don't know, Mom," Amelia said. "I honestly don't. I'm in a hotel or a condo or something…"

"A hotel," Jake added.

"Oh, good to know that much. I'm in a hotel," Amelia continued. She turned to Jake. "Is this still Las Vegas?" she asked.

"North Las Vegas, yes," he replied.

"Nevada?" Amelia asked.

"Yes, there's only one Las Vegas and North Las Vegas, as far as I know," Jake said. "We're definitely in Nevada."

"Good Lord, Amelia," Diane said. "How did you get to the northern part of the city without realizing it? I guess that means you didn't drive there yourself. And how have three days passed without your knowledge? Daughter, are you in trouble?"

Before Amelia could answer her mom's questions, she heard a ripping and buckling noise coming from outside the door. It was Michael again. He was back, and he was determined to get inside. The metal door creaked and bent until it burst off its hinges, falling against its frame and dangling from the chain, which still did not budge. Michael stepped inside, tossing what looked like a crowbar onto the floor beside him. Satisfied with his grand entrance, he turned his attention to Amelia and Jake.

"Hi, sir," Jake tried. "I deliver room service here at the hotel. I brought the breakfast you ordered…"

Michael scowled, walking slowly and deliberately towards them. He was livid, his face red as blood. He didn't speak a word. Amelia shuddered. Jake cocked his head, working hard to think of something to say that would talk Michael down. Nothing could.

"She wanted to make a phone call, so I helped her dial an outside line," Jake continued. "It's tricky sometimes. You have to dial another digit first, and people sometimes forget which one…"

Michael stopped just arm's length away from both Amelia and Jake. He stood stoically for a moment, still and silent. Then, in what can only be described as the actions of a madman, Michael grabbed the edge of the sheet from under Amelia's arms. Moving rapidly and using the sheet to cover his hands, he took the phone receiver from Amelia and ripped it from its base, disconnecting the call with Diane. Moving too fast for either Amelia or Jake to react, Michael lifted the receiver high above Jake's innocent head. He brought it down at a dizzying speed, striking Jake repeatedly and from all angles. Michael looked like a boxer delivering the winning blows in the ring, only there were no rules or officials to keep him from going too far.

Jake was knocked unconscious as Amelia looked on in horror. His lifeless body fell on the floor in a heap. Michael dropped to his knees beside Jake and continued his assault, relentlessly striking the young man. Soon, Jake's breathing stopped and his eyes became vacant.

He was gone, murdered at Michael's hands.

"What did you do?" Amelia asked, disgusted.

Michael shifted his weight back, then dropped the sheet and the phone onto the floor.

"I didn't do this," he said smugly, wiping perspiration from his brow. "You did. Your fingerprints are all over the phone. Now put the damn dress on and meet me downstairs, before you end up like your little friend."

17

**Present Day
Rosemary Run, California**

Marcheline stood tall on the bench in front of the crowd, focusing all of her attention on the task at hand. A woman was in grave danger. Amelia needed real, results-oriented help. Marcheline intended to provide exactly that. The quest was personal now.

"Let's begin by taking stock of what we know," Marcheline said. "First, the young woman's name. Amelia. Does anyone here know her last name? The woman with her was Rebecca Tatum, Officer James Tatum's wife. Rebecca courageously got into the back of the pickup truck with another good samaritan before the vehicle sped away. We need to assume that all three of them are in jeopardy."

At first, no one answered. There were blank stares and frustrated expressions. The crowd wanted to offer some scrap of information that would be useful, but nothing was coming to the surface.

"Anything at all?" Marcheline said. "Even the smallest piece of information could be relevant."

"My date-- er, boyfriend, I guess-- is the guy who got into the back of the pickup truck, too," a clean cut man in a sweater vest and slacks said. "His name is Shane Baxter. He's a retired Marine. We haven't known each other all that long, but I suspect he has skills and training that will come in handy."

Marcheline smiled at the man. "Thank you, sir, and hats off to your boyfriend. He's shown extraordinary bravery today. What is your name?"

"I'm Marty. Marty Douglas."

"Hello, Marty," Marcheline replied.

"I'm from the Northwestern side of the Bay Area," he continued. "Petaluma. I wish I could be of more help."

Marcheline nodded. Julien pulled out his smartphone and began to take notes. "I'll record everything we know," he said softly to his wife. "Go ahead. I'm getting it all."

"Wait," Bill said, the wheels in his mind obviously turning. "I got a call from a woman last summer whose daughter was named Amelia."

Marcheline turned to him, hopeful. Bill had continued his private investigative business on the side even after coming to work at Maison du Vin. He had enjoyed the challenge PI clients brought, and he was good at it. He'd thought it would have been a shame to let all of his years of experience go to waste.

"That might be something, Bill," Marcheline said. "Do you have a last name?"

All eyes fixed on him as he searched his memory. "Butcher," I think. "No, Baker. Yes, that's it. Baker! Amelia Baker."

A few people clapped spontaneously.

"Good," Marcheline said. "Do you have any other information on her?"

"It's generally considered confidential if I do," Bill replied.

Marcheline gave him a look that said he had better make an exception.

"I get it," he said. "Her safety trumps that confidentiality. We have to rescue her. I'm sure I have my notes somewhere with all of the details."

"But where?" Rande asked. "I know you're an old school pen and paper kind of guy, Bill. We don't have the time for you to go back to your home office and dig through a filing cabinet. We need information now."

Bill nodded. "I agree. Let me look through emails on my phone. Her mother emailed me the first time we interacted. I don't remember for sure, but I believe she may have sent me her phone number in that email."

"Brilliant!" Marcheline said, getting excited. "If we can contact Amelia's mom, we can learn so much more."

"Hopefully," Rande said.

"What do you mean?" Marcheline asked her friend. "What are you thinking, Rande?"

"I'm thinking we need to focus on learning more about the guy that took her out of here by the hair. What do we know about him?"

"I got the license plate number!" someone shouted. "Me, too!" said another.

"Our new friend, Blanca, has it as well," Marcheline said. "She's on her way to the police station with that information now. Good work to all of you who took note of the number. You're brave and kind, all of you."

Rande paced back and forth as he thought. "Without police here, we've got to move forward on our own. We can't just wait. Not if we want to save that lady."

"We have a police scanner," Marcheline added. "Blanca brought it from her car. She said it was easy to use."

"That's a start," Rande said. "Someone should listen to try and find out what's holding them up."

"Any volunteers?" Marcheline asked.

Marty's hand shot up. "I'll do it," he said.

"Wonderful!" Marcheline exclaimed.

Rande walked Marty to a nearby supply room and got him situated at a makeshift table with paper, a pencil, and the scanner.

"Take notes," Rande said. "We need to know where the police are. And where they aren't. Anything you can glean is great. Come get me if you hear something that sounds important."

Marty nodded, proud to be of use. Marcheline continued the meeting out front.

"What else?" she asked no one in particular. "We can search for them ourselves if we can figure out where to look."

Seemingly oblivious to everything else around him, Bill jumped and pumped his fist in the air. "Found it! He said. Diane Baker, Amelia's mom. I have her phone number."

A murmur spread across the crowd. Finally, they were getting somewhere.

"Call her!" someone shouted.

"Yes, call her," Marcheline confirmed. "Right away. Go into the janitor's closet, next to the supply room. Take notes. Find out everything you can."

Bill nodded, reaching into one pocket and pulling out a stylus that worked with his smartphone. "I'll make notes on here!" he said. "On my way."

Marcheline breathed a sigh of relief. They were making excellent progress. How fortunate that Amelia's mom had contacted Bill last summer. That probably meant she'd suspected Michael of something. Otherwise, she wouldn't have contacted a private investigator.

"Very good," Marcheline said. "What else can we do? Who else do we know?"

A woman stepped forward. "I know Detective Neil Fredericks of the Rosemary Run Police Department," she said. "His kids took swimming lessons with mine this past summer. We carpooled. I have his mobile number. And he's married to Officer James Tatum's sister."

"Excellent," Marcheline said. "Will you call him, please? Tell him what has happened, and be sure to let him know that James' wife, Rebecca, is involved. He'll want to get word to James right away."

The woman stepped back again, a proud expression on her face. She pushed a few buttons on her mobile phone, then lifted it to her ear. The pieces and parts of this puzzle would surely fit together soon.

Before Marcheline could prompt the group again, Leigh, the Maison du Vin employee who'd had the unfortunate chance to encounter Michael at the hostess stand, came running out of the restaurant. She was holding something in her hand.

"I found her phone!" Leigh shouted cheerfully.

The crowd gasped. Things were on track now. And this was a big development.

"Good work, Leigh!" Marcheline said, a big smile on her face. "I'm so happy to hear this. Where did you find it?"

"It was folded up in the tablecloth that had fallen on the floor inside," Leigh explained. "She doesn't even keep it locked. I checked, and we can access the device. Lucky, right?"

"You can say that again," Rande says with a chuckle. "If you don't mind, Leigh, I'll take a look."

"Sure thing," Leigh replied, placing the phone in Rande's hand.

Her cheeks were flushed from the physical exertion. She smiled as she brushed strands of blonde hair out of her face. It was good for them all to work together. They knew themselves to be productive and useful. Being able to help was a wonderful feeling.

"Let's see what we have," Rande said as he looked through Amelia's phone. "Oh, look at that. She and her friend-- Rebecca, right?-- they took a photo together sitting on this very bench. It appears to have been taken earlier today. Is this what they were wearing?"

Marcheline studied the photo as Rande held it up towards her. "Yes, I believe so," she said.

"So, we know for sure this phone belongs to Amelia Baker," Rande confirmed. "That's a good place to start."

"Look at her recent calls," Julien suggested, a look of concern on his face. "The man who took her away probably called her first. That would make sense, yes?"

"You're exactly right, Julien," Marcheline said.

"And if we can find his mobile phone number, the mobile phone company can track it," Rande added.

"But won't that take a long time?" Marty asked. "I'd try and track Shane's phone, but he left it in the car so it wouldn't interfere with our lunch. I'm the one who suggested that, and now I wish I hadn't."

"That's quite alright," Marcheline said. "Don't feel badly, Marty. We'll use what we have. We'll keep trying the police, and we'll call the mobile phone company to enlist their help."

"I can do you one better," Rande said, smiling like a cat who had just eaten a canary. "Just as Julien suspected, Amelia's phone received seventeen missed calls from the same number leading up to the drama here today. Amelia has the number saved with the name Michael Bell. As luck would have it, location sharing is enabled for Michael's number. I'm looking at his location right now."

"Are you serious?" Julien said. "Wow! Rande, that's amazing."

"You're a good one, my darling," Marcheline said to Rande. "Nice work. Where are they?"

"Not far outside of town," Rande replied. "Looks like they're at a scrap yard heading towards the mountain. I believe I've been there before."

"Let's go!" someone shouted from the back. "I know that place, too."

"Best I can figure, he's ditching his truck for a new

one," Rande added. "Which means we need to move fast. It will be much harder to find them without a plate number and vehicle description."

"On it!" someone else said. "If that's where she is, then I'm going. Let's rescue Amelia!"

Just then, Bill emerged from the building, smiling broadly.

"Get her?" Marcheline asked.

"You bet I did," Bill replied. "I spoke with Diane. She's on her way, awaiting our specific instructions."

"Fabulous," Marcheline said.

"And that's not all," Bill added. "Diane says she's bringing Amelia's ex-boyfriend, Troy Weeks. Apparently, the guy has been worried sick about Amelia for quite some time now. Just yesterday, Amelia left him a voicemail telling him that she was in trouble. He's amped up and ready to whatever is necessary to get her away from that monster."

"Thank the heavens," Marcheline said, tipping her head up to the sky. "Well, you can call Diane right back," she continued, "because we believe we've tracked his phone. We're on our way."

Bill nodded happily, already dialing Diane. Marty heard the happy uproar and emerged from the building as well. Before he could report on what he'd heard on the scanner, the group's conversation was interrupted by the wailing of police sirens. Three squad cars raced into the Maison du Vin parking lot, gravel flying behind them. James Tatum was in the lead, another uniformed officer riding shotgun. He parked his car hastily and leaped out. His chiseled features looked strong and determined.

"My wife?" he asked. "Rebecca Tatum. Where is she?"

James didn't bother to introduce himself to Marcheline or to confirm that she was the owner of Maison du Vin. They'd met before, in passing. James' focus was on his wife. Marcheline understood that. She'd feel the same way in his shoes.

"We think we've tracked them," Marcheline said, cutting right to the chase. She wanted to ask James what had taken them so long, but she didn't. There would be time to talk in more detail once Amelia, Rebecca, and Shane were found safe and rescued. "We can go now," she continued, "it appears they're at a junkyard, not far out of town."

"Rebecca is there, too?" James asked.

Officers got out of the other two cars now. They were an eager bunch, all bright eyed and bushy tailed. *Thank God*, Marcheline thought. They appeared to already know that James' wife was involved, and they supported him completely. They had the distinct look of a group that wouldn't let each other down. Marcheline had heard that about the Rosemary Run Police Department. They had a reputation as a tight knit force. She assumed that Officer Fredericks would show up any minute as well.

"Yes," Marcheline confirmed. "Rebecca is with her friend, Amelia Baker. I presume you know her."

"Of course, I do. They've been best friends for years. But this was called in as a domestic disturbance," James said. "Was that Amelia? Her husband?"

"If you can call him that," Julien replied. "He's a sorry excuse for a husband, as far as I'm concerned."

James nodded. He didn't seem all that surprised to hear that Michael was the perpetrator.

"He made quite a scene in our restaurant," Marcheline said. "He dragged Amelia out of here, literally kicking and screaming. I'm licensed to carry a weapon, and I had it out to take aim. I couldn't get a shot off safely, though. I felt I had no choice but to let them go."

James nodded again. He wasn't in the mood for long explanations.

"Here's where we think they are, Officer," Rande said, showing James the screen. "This is Amelia's phone. She left it in our restaurant. This number is saved in her device as Michael Bell. And location services are turned on. She was tracking him, and good thing, too. It might just save her life."

"And Rebecca's," James said softly. He stood for a moment, getting his bearings. "Good work, folks," he said as he tipped his hat towards the crowd. "We're in pursuit."

James tilted his head and spoke rapidly into the radio affixed to a shoulder strap on his uniform. He told the dispatcher where the junkyard was located and what they knew so far.

"My boyfriend is there, too," Marty added. "Shane Baxter. He got into the back of the truck with Rebecca."

"Wait," James said. "Rebecca got in voluntarily?"

Marcheline smiled. "That, she did. She's a brave one. You're a lucky man."

James chuckled a little and shook his head. "Okay," she said, focusing on the details at hand. He spoke into his radio once more. "Michael Bell apparently took his wife, Amelia Baker, against her will. Rebecca Tatum and Shane

Baxter voluntarily got into the back of Mr. Bell's truck to try and save Amelia."

Marcheline nodded to let him know he had the details right.

"Someone will let you know what happens," James said as he opened the door of his squad car to get in.

"That won't be necessary," Marchline said. "We're going with you."

"You can't…" James began, then thought better of it. "You know what? I won't try to stop you. Please, just don't make me regret saying that. Whatever you do, be smart about it. I have a hunch you will, Ms. Fay."

Marcheline raised her hand to her forehead in a makeshift salute. "Yes, sir, Officer Tatum. We promise to do only good. No harm. We'll see you out there."

18

Present Day
Rosemary Run, California

Michael Bell had deceived Amelia in the worst possible way. From the moment he had walked into that bar where she sat stirring her mixed drink while feeling dejected and alone, he had pretended to care for her. He hadn't really. Amelia was a means to an end. A target. A relationship of convenience.

Sure, he had found her attractive. It hadn't hurt that she was eye candy, and she was good in bed. She had tolerated some of his sexual kinks with minimal complaints. But he'd never wanted Amelia to be a part of his future beyond the time it would take to expand his criminal enterprise into Northern California. Michael had no interest in any real or true personal connections. To him, life was a game and the people in it were merely pawns to move around as he pleased.

When Michael had set his sights on Amelia, the

business climate in Las Vegas had been cooling as a result of a turf war in nearby Southern California. It had made everyone in the business more jumpy than usual. They hadn't challenged Michael's status as top dog in Sin City, but it had become more and more difficult to operate in the shadows as investigators leveraged feuding bosses to squeeze information out of lesser players. Vegas police had been on Michael's trail. It had been time for him to make a move or risk everything he'd built. He'd needed to expand in an area that was quieter and lower profile. He'd need to hide in plain sight.

Michael had thought it would be easy. He'd find a gullible woman from a small town to provide a convincing cover story. Then he'd establish a new, wider network and expand his money laundering operation in an inconspicuous location. Amelia had fit the bill to a tee.

Unluckily for her, the gritty motorcycle dude from rural Missouri she'd slept with earlier in her vacation had tipped Michael off. The man had been a scout of sorts, helping Michael sift through vulnerable women for just the right mark. Once he'd found Amelia, he'd shared the relevant details. All Michael'd had to do was show up and charm her. Easy peasy. It had been like taking candy from a baby, just as he'd expected.

On day one, Amelia had talked of her dream wedding and visions of a self discovery quest like she'd read about in some half-baked chick lit memoirs. Not to mention, it had been plain to see how prancing around and feeling sexually desirable gave her a sense of control over her broken, pitiful life. All Michael had needed to do was to listen attentively to Amelia's musings, pump her full of alcohol, then claim that they'd gotten married. It hadn't mattered that she didn't remember the imaginary ceremony. They hadn't really married. But the suggestion had been enough to force a real wedding in Rosemary Run with Amelia's friends and family a few months later.

Michael was a master at grooming women. He knew how to move slowly enough that they had some sense of security. And he knew how to strike suddenly when it was time to go in for the kill. He'd done exactly that with Amelia, easing her in then testing the limits of her loyalty.

Jake Webber, the room service guy, had been collateral damage. Michael hadn't intended to end the young man's life, but in hindsight, he decided that turn of events had worked in his favor. Once Michael had framed the murder as Amelia's fault, he'd had her exactly where he'd wanted her. She had been stuck. He'd threatened to turn her into the authorities if she dared go against him. After all, her fingerprints had been on the telephone receiver that was used to bludgeon the man.

With the help of Michael's various associates including Big Jim Byers and Omar Cox, he could make anything go his way. They and others would provide any assistance or diversion Michael might need. He'd had a number of dangerous men at his beck and call. It hadn't hurt that Amelia's best friend was married to a cop either. Michael had used James Tatum as an ongoing threat. He'd promised to tell James all about how Amelia had murdered Jake if she'd even thought about crossing him. As for her mother, Diane, well, she'd had her grievances with Michael, but he'd managed to play the part of doting husband whenever she was around. He'd convinced Diane that Amelia's ramblings on the telephone the day Jake called had been the result of a wicked hangover after a night out partying. She'd been none the wiser. At least, so Michael had thought.

He'd had everything planned. Every detail had been calculated and accounted for. Amelia had been too vulnerable to fight back. She'd felt like she deserved the abuse Michael dished out, and a woman in that frame of mind was easy to control.

What Michael hadn't counted on was how close knit the Rosemary Run community was. He'd let his temper flare in public, and now they'd rallied together to bring him down. Maybe Amelia had gone into a public establishment that day because she knew the community would come to her aid. Maybe it had been a huge cry for help. Maybe she had even chosen Marcheline Fay's establishment because she had known that Marcheline was a survivor of abuse herself. Amelia had read Marcheline's story in the newspaper. She knew that Marcheline had found a strength in facing her personal demons and not letting them define her. If Amelia's choice of Maison du Vin had been deliberate, she'd done the right thing. Now, she had lots of help. All the help she'd need.

There was a palpable energy in the air as the caravan of rescue vehicles made their way along the winding roads leading to the junk yard where Amelia, Rebecca, and Shane waited. James led the charge in his police car, lights flashing. He kept the sirens off so as not to alert Michael to his approach, but he'd turn them on later. The two other police cruisers in his company followed, as did an ambulance and an unmarked police car driven by Detective Neil Fredericks and his partner, Detective Luke Hemming. The civilian squad filed in close behind. Marcheline, Julian, Rande, Bill, and Marty rode together in Marcheline's SUV. Blanca drove her car with several ridealong bystanders from the crowd. Diane and Troy joined in at the back of the line, although Glada, the rideshare driver, had a police scanner of her own and had heard about the commotion. She'd driven Amelia and Rebecca to Maison du Vin earlier in the day and wanted to do her part to save them. She jumped in behind Diane as a last minute add-on to the convoy.

The sheer number of people joined together to help was awe inspiring. With that many folks standing together, surely, they would bring their fellow friends and neighbors home safely. They wouldn't stand for bad behavior like this in their community. Rosemary Run had seen the likes of organized crime before. James' brother-in-law, Mick, had even gotten mixed up in it. But that had only made the town more steadfast about putting an end to such bad actors before they could grow powerful and take permanent hold.

By the time James turned on his sirens and pulled onto the dirt road leading to the junkyard, the situation had become dire for Amelia, Rebecca, and Shane.

A short time before, Byers had come around the front of the truck to check on Amelia while Michael checked out a motor home at the back of the property. Realizing Amelia was unconscious and not just sleeping, Byers had pulled her out of the vehicle, thinking he might have needed to perform CPR. She'd come to when he'd moved her, which had been a relief to them all. But that hadn't been the end of the story. In fact, that's where things had gone off the rails.

Byers had discovered Rebecca and Shane in the bed of the truck. He'd had a choice at that juncture. He could have called the authorities and been on the right side of the law. But the big man hadn't. Instead, he'd shouted to Michael, alerting him to the presence of the stowaways. Not to mention, Byers had been heavily armed. When he had confronted Shane and Rebecca, it had been from the other end of a seriously large gun. They'd had no real option but to do what he'd said. Despite all of their courage and their desire to be heroes, Shane and Rebecca found themselves tied to scummy chairs in the dingy mobile home that housed the junkyard office. Amelia was also tied, but to a table in the back. She had been too weak to sit upright. It was in those positions the three of them remained when the rescue vehicles streamed onto the property, lights flashing, sirens blaring, and guns blazing.

What happened next occured in a flash of moving bodies and flying bullets. Police streamed in with a furious intensity and a clumsy fire fight ensued.

One female officer took a bullet to the chest that had been fired by Byers. Thanks to her bullet-proof vest, she survived the hit winded, but unscathed. Byers, on the other hand, wasn't so fortunate. He took a nasty shot to the neck that caused him to bleed out before paramedics could do anything to help. He was gone within minutes.

Seeing this, Michael barricaded himself in a small store room. No one was sure what his strategy was. He didn't last long in that spot, what with so many people who wanted to see him pay. When it became clear he was out of bullets, the crowd literally disassembled the room around Michael. He sat stoically, waiting to face his fate. Gone were the tantrums, the rage, and the dominance. He was outnumbered now. His attitude was that of a predator who had finally met his match in the form of a protective herd. Michael might have won in a fight against any one of them, but together, they were mightier than he could ever be alone.

An officer arrested Michael unceremoniously and put him into the back of a police car. Finally, the monster had been put in a cage. And without a big show of it to boot.

With Byers down and Michael secured, everyone turned their attention to the rescues. James rushed to Rebecca, untying her and enveloping her in his strong arms. Marty did the same for Shane, planting a grateful kiss on his boyfriend's lips.

"You're my hero, you know," Marty whispered.

"Not even," Shane replied. "We didn't have a chance to do anything. We were just getting plans together when we ended up tied here. It was all very anticlimactic."

"Not so," Marty said. "You two jumped in the truck bed, risking your own safety and ready to help. You'll always be heroes in my book."

James smiled at his wife, stroking her hair gently. "I'll have to agree. You two are heroes, indeed. The best."

"The very, very best, my darlings. Each of you," Marcheline added, looking like a proud mama bear as she surveyed the scene.

From her vantage point on the table in the office,

Amelia couldn't tell what was happening. She had been so traumatized, so confused, and in so much pain that she could scarcely keep up with where she was. She knew that Michael had taken her somewhere. She remembered him causing a big scene and yelling like a madman at Maison du Vin. But she thought she'd heard Rebecca's voice. She'd known that couldn't be right. Or could it?

The next thing Amelia knew, her mom's face was in front of hers. Strangers were gathered around her, too. It was all a blur. Her awareness was fuzzy. Were they here to help her? She blinked her eyes, moving in and out of consciousness. She couldn't quite figure out how or why her mom would be there, but she was glad. Forcing herself to wake up, if only just for a minute, Amelia finally opened her eyes long enough to see clearly. It was her mom, alright. And a team of medics. *Thank God almighty*, she thought. She knew she needed to get to a hospital and be seen by a doctor.

"Honey, he's been arrested," Diane said. "You're safe. He won't hurt you ever again."

"Really?" Amelia asked. "You know what he did to me? What he was doing to me?"

"We don't know everything, but we know enough," Diane said. "It's all okay now, though. When you're better, you can talk to the police and tell them the details. We'll get it sorted out. I'll be right with you every step of the way. If you want me to be, that is..."

Amelia nodded feebly. She *did* want her mom to be there with her. She was happy to see her now, and she hoped that they could start a new chapter in their relationship.

"Bec? Where is she?"

"She's here, too," Diane said. "In the other room with James. There's someone else who wants to see you."

"Okay," Amelia said.

She was tired, and the paramedics were poking and prodding her. She couldn't imagine who else would want to see her now. Especially here, like this. Then Diane moved back and Troy stepped into view. His round features danced with delight like they always did at the sight of her.

"Hey you," he said as he clasped one of her hands in his. "How's my best girl?"

"Troy?" Amelia asked, with all the enthusiasm she could muster. "You're here."

They both smiled. Even though it had been a long, hard road, the two of them maintained a deep affection for each other. Even though there was much to discuss and even more to disclose, at a fundamental level, Amelia and Troy knew that what they shared had endured the unthinkable. There was no good reason it couldn't go on to endure whatever else life had in store. They would face what came next together-- Amelia, Troy, their families and friends, and the good people of charming and scenic Rosemary Run, California.

Troy's response to the love of his life said it all. "No place I'd rather be."

THE END.

———

Get the next book in the series:

Her Silent Misery
Rosemary Run - Book Seven

———

BONUS CONTENT -

Rosemary Run Short Story

Get a FREE prequel short story exclusively when you sign up for Kelly's email newsletter:

Her Troubled Mind

ENJOY THIS BOOK?

A NOTE FROM AUTHOR KELLY UTT

Did you enjoy this book? You can make a big difference.

Honest reviews of my books help bring them to the attention of other readers.

If you've enjoyed this book, I would be very grateful if you could spend just five minutes leaving a review (it can be as short as you like) on the book's retail page where you purchased and on Goodreads or BookBub.

Thank you very much.

ABOUT THE AUTHOR

STANDARDS OF STARLIGHT BOOKS
KELLY UTT

Kelly Utt writes emotional thrillers for readers who enjoy both suspense and sentimentality. She was born in Youngstown, Ohio in 1976.

Kelly grew up with a dad who would read a book on a weighty topic, ask her to read it, too, and then insist they discuss it together, igniting her passion for life's big questions. That passion is often reflected inKelly's novels, giving them a depth which leaves readers wanting more and thinking about her stories long after the last lines are read.

Kelly holds a Bachelor's degree in psychology from the

University of Tennessee, Knoxville and she studied graduate-level interactive media at Quinnipiac University.

She lives in Nashville, Tennessee with her husband and sons. She also writes romance as Corena Kelly.

www.kellyutt.com

www.ingramcontent.com/pod-product-compliance
Lightning Source LLC
Chambersburg PA
CBHW071804190726
48292CB00008B/2703